Knitting Can Walk!

Lance Greenfield

This is for the real Knitting, who inspired this
story and has continued to be an inspiration
to us all

First Kindle Edition, January 2016
First Lulu Edition, February 2016
Copyright © Lance Greenfield 2016

Edited by Eloise de Sousa
Cover design by Lance Greenfield

ISBN: 978-1-326-46392-2
ASIN: B017BVQVAI

This is a work of fiction. Names, characters, places and incidents are either products of the author's imagination or are used fictitiously, and any resemblance to actual persons, living or dead, or to actual events or locales is entirely coincidental.

If you want happiness for an hour, take a nap.
If you want happiness for a day, go fishing.
If you want happiness for a month, get married.
If you want happiness for a year, inherit a fortune.
If you want happiness for a lifetime, help somebody else.

Chinese proverb - Anon.

"You don't learn to walk by following rules. You learn by doing and falling over."

Richard Branson

Acknowledgements

The background for this story came from some of my own teenage experiences which I have embellished to create a much more lively work of fiction than the true facts of my life at that time would ever achieve. So there are a few, very tiny fragments of truth in this story, but over ninety percent of it has been made up. If, by any chance, you are a friend or acquaintance of mine from my young adult days and think that you recognise yourself in this tale, then you are sadly mistaken.

This book has been edited by my friend and fellow author, Eloise De Sousa, whom I met online during the NaNoWriMo challenge in November 2014 as I was writing my debut novel, *Eleven Miles*. I thank her for all her efforts in eliminating my silly mistakes and for providing great advice on the structure and pace of this story. I am also very grateful to the NaNoWriMo community for motivating me to believe in myself enough to produce a novel in a month.

I would also thank my many friends and family who have encouraged me to get on with writing a second novel when I most needed their motivation.

Other books by Lance Greenfield

Eleven Miles (2014)

Prologue

Panchali Masih was full of admiration as she stared across her desk at the smartly turned-out man in front of her. She had already made her decision. Calum McDougal was perfect. She would definitely offer him the role of Global Customer Services Director at Summit Software. From the moment he walked through the door that morning, he had impressed everyone that he encountered. People had been running into the CEO's office all day to tell her that they would love to welcome Calum to the senior management team of the company.

Indeed, Calum had gained Panchali's immediate respect during that first breakfast meeting in the Savoy Hotel in London back in December. She'd had no hesitation in inviting him to New Jersey for a round of second and final interviews. The shortlist had been down to only two candidates, but his rival for the post had been almost a standard, stereotypical senior manager. Calum was something special.

However, she felt compelled to interview him. She doubted if he would blow his chances at this late stage, but it could happen. She had a feeling that she was about to enjoy the experience.

Calum sat comfortably and smiled back at Panchali. It was obvious that he would not speak until he had been spoken to. She glanced down at the CV and notes in front of her.

"It's been a long day for you. You've met with all my senior managers and a lot of the staff. And you gave a great presentation this morning." She paused. "So, after all that, what do you think of my company?"

Calum considered his answer carefully before responding. He didn't want to upset the owner of this company, because he really wanted the job. It had been a wonderful day once the shock of the initial encounter with the VP of Human Resources had worn off. He had met Licia in the car park shortly before eight o'clock. She had asked him how he would like to set up his presentation. "It will be in the boardroom, of course. We have a projector and a screen if you have slides on your laptop to show. We even have an old-fashioned overhead projector if you've brought some transparencies!" She'd laughed as she made this last remark.

"What do you mean by MY presentation, Licia?"

"Your presentation on 'How Summit Software will gain a beach-head in Europe,' of course."

A look of shocked realisation had broken across Calum's face. "Oh no! I'm sorry. I looked at your agenda and was expecting to watch one of your executives presenting that case for my benefit."

"Oh dear. There's obviously been a misunderstanding, Calum. I do apologise. It must be my fault. The agenda is ambiguous. I should have written the owners' names against each agenda item. I'd better tell Panchali about my mistake immediately. She's expecting you to brief us on how you'd get the business going across the pond. We'll have to cancel that session." Licia was obviously distressed by her error. "Oh dear. She's not going to be too happy with me for this."

Thinking quickly, Calum saw that all was not lost. He might even turn it to his advantage.

"It's alright, Licia. If you could explain the situation to Panchali and ask her if I can have until nine to prepare, I am sure that I can come up with something in that time. It's an hour-long session, so I only need four or five slides as background to my talk. I'll just tell everyone about my ideas on the matter and open up a general discussion. I could benefit from the vast experience in the room, and I am not going to be running alone in Europe. I'm sure that

I'll have plenty of advice and support from the leadership team."

"Are you sure? You've already got less than an hour to prepare."

"Yes. No problem. Just tell me where I can sit in peace for a while, and point me to the coffee machine."

"You can sit in the boardroom. Nobody will disturb you. And the coffee's right here," she said, pointing to the open kitchen door.

At five to nine, people had started coming into the boardroom, introducing themselves briefly as they took their seats. By the time Panchali had joined the assembly, there were twenty-two men and women sitting expectantly around the large table. The CEO took control and asked Calum to launch straight into his presentation, as they were already running half an hour behind schedule.

The audience listened respectfully as Calum talked to them about the likely target organisational structure in Europe, which would initially be run out of the United Kingdom, developing the small existing customer base, the creation of likely partners and their enablement, training for staff, customers and partners and the support that he would expect from the much larger team in the USA.

As he had expected, there were a lot of questions, which he thought he fielded quite well, and much discussion. There was a very friendly, receptive atmosphere in the room. He could tell that his well-tested ploy of switching from "I would..." to "we will..." half way through the presentation had paid off handsomely. They were already speaking to him as if he were part of the team.

Throughout the discussion, Panchali had remained silent and relaxed at the far end of the table. She was keenly observing every move and every word.

Finally, she asked a question.

"Say I were to give you the job right now. What would be your first action, back in London, next Monday?"

Calum didn't even have to think about his answer for one second. He already knew.

"The job title says it all. I would be the first appointed Global Customer Services Director at Summit Software. Naturally, my job would be founded upon the services that our customers require, or believe they require. I would plan, and embark upon, a whistle-stop tour of ALL of our existing customers, worldwide. In advance, I would make sure that the most appropriate senior contacts within each of our customers could make themselves available to spend some time with me during my visits. I'd need some assistance to do that. I would ask them all to lay it on the line for me: the good, the bad and the ugly of their interactions with Summit Software. I would listen very carefully to their perceptions of us. I would be asking them what more we could do for them, and doing my best to spot opportunities to deliver more services and better services to them all. I'd need some admin support to plan all of this, but I would aggressively drive my own timescales so that I could get back to London and plan our next moves as soon as possible. My guess is that, within six to eight weeks, we'd have a very good idea of what would be required, and we could then prioritise, taking into account our current capabilities and budgets."

The room was silent. Calum wondered for a moment if he had got it completely wrong. Most of the management team were turning to look at their CEO.

Panchali leaned forward and applauded. She actually applauded! The rest of the audience joined her.

"Calum. I have to tell you that I could not have heard a better answer to that question if I had written it myself!"

Once everybody except Licia and Calum had left the room, Licia beamed broadly and offered her congratulations on a great performance. She then offered to take Calum to his first one-to-one meeting, which would be with Kumar, the Chief Technology Officer. "I was really worried for you this morning, when we discovered the misunderstanding about the presentation. I'm amazed that you pulled it off so well."

"Thanks Licia. I actually work best when I present on the fly. Months of preparation for a presentation makes it go kind of flat, don't you think?"

For the rest of the day, Calum had enjoyed a succession of thirty-minute meetings with all of the senior managers. What he had most enjoyed was the informality of the lunch break. He had sat with the developers, support team and administrators as they shared their lunch boxes that they'd all prepared and brought in to work. He loved this culture. Most amusing was the short cricket match that followed lunch. The American colleagues were obviously quite bemused by the strange game that the Indians were playing outside on the grass. Calum tried to explain it away as "a bit like baseball, but with only two bases and two batters." That had confused the locals even more.

At last, he had reached the final interview of the day; of the whole process. He knew that answering Panchali's question regarding his thoughts on her company honestly could carry a potentially huge risk, but being straightforward and truthful, despite the risks involved, had usually paid enormous dividends. He decided to go for it.

"To be honest, I love your company, its products and its people, and I feel that I could really fit in here, but I think that your trademark is actually worth more than your entire company. If Bill Gates or Larry Ellison or any other IT giant wanted to print those three little words on any of their boxes, they would have to pay Summit Software an absolute fortune for the privilege."

There was a long pause as Panchali stared at him, looking very serious. He wondered if he'd made a big mistake. Eventually, she smiled.

Calum was very relieved when Panchali's smile broadened into a grin. She laughed.

"That is very perceptive of you, Calum. And you are very brave to say it to my face. Others may have thought it in the past, but nobody has ever been bold enough to say that to me before. It is my turn to be honest with you now. What you just told me is precisely the reason that the trademark is registered in my own personal name rather than in the company's name."

Panchali lowered her gaze to Calum's CV once more.

"I see that you are interested in mathematical puzzles. Does that include the ones made of blocks of wood, pieces of string and wires?"

"Yes. They're great fun."

She reached down to pick up a large wooden box from the side of her desk. Tipping the contents noisily onto the surface she challenged, "Good! I love them too. Have a go at some of these while we speak."

Calum scanned the puzzles before him. There were several with which he was already very familiar. He quickly grabbed one of his favourites and started to take it apart. As he did so, he informed Panchali that some of his favourite books when he was a youngster had been Martin Gardner's *Mathematical Puzzles and Diversions* series.

She chuckled. "Me too!"

Calum nimbly finished the first puzzle and picked up another.

The questioning moved on to much more business-focused concepts, especially back onto the morning's topic of how Calum saw the business running in Europe and how he expected to develop the services team and business worldwide. All the time that they were speaking, he continued to dismantle the puzzles. Panchali could see what he was doing and selected one that she knew was unique. It had been designed and crafted by her grandfather, just for her, when she'd been about ten years old.

Calum struggled with it, eventually daring to pass it back to the CEO with a request that she show him the trick. She was delighted to do so, and even more delighted when Calum had no trouble in repeating the solution a few seconds later.

"You are a very open and honest person Calum, and I like that. All of my executives, and all of the junior staff that I have spoken to during the day like you very much. I want to be equally open and honest with you now. For the last half an hour I have been observing you. You already had the job when you walked in this morning. I just wanted to go through the interview with you as confirmation of my initial thoughts. Have you enjoyed the day and the whole process?"

"I have, Panchali, very much. But does this mean that you are offering me the job?"

"Yes it does. I want you to work here at Summit Software. Licia has already drafted an offer letter for you, which I'd like you to take away with you. I am sure that you will find the terms to be very appealing to you, but I am open to negotiation if you wish to discuss any of the details. You can tell me your answer tomorrow morning before you depart for the airport, or you can take it back to England and call me next week. Perhaps you'd like time to discuss it with your family?"

"No. That won't be necessary. I wouldn't have made the trip here if my wife hadn't been as enthusiastic as I am about the job and this company. Today has just reinforced my feelings. I'll read the offer, but I am almost certain that I will be in here to accept first thing tomorrow morning."

"Great! However, before we finish for the day, there is one more question that I always like to ask every interviewee. I am afraid that it is somewhat of an interview cliché, but I am keen to discover what your answer will be.

I have a feeling I might hear something new from you."
She paused. Calum frowned. "What would you say has
been the greatest achievement of your life so far?"

"That is very easy for me to answer, Panchali. There is
no doubt whatsoever that the greatest achievement of my
life so far, and I know that I will never surpass this if I live
to be a hundred, is that I taught a little girl to walk after the
clinical experts had declared that she would never be able
to walk."

For once in her life, Panchali was genuinely stunned.
She was speechless as she tried to absorb Calum's
statement. Her mouth actually hung open.

"Say that again!"

"I taught a little girl, a six-year-old Chinese orphan
girl, to walk, despite the advice from top clinical experts in
Hong Kong that it would never be possible for her to walk
on her own."

"If you are telling me what I think I just heard, then
this is truly amazing. Almost incredible. Please tell me
more."

"Do you want to hear the short version or the long
version?"

Panchali considered this for a few moments.

"Calum. If you don't have any plans for this evening,
my family and I would be delighted if you would dine with
us and tell us all about this little girl who learned to walk.
Would you please join us?"

"Yes. I'd love to accept your generous invitation. I was
only going to sit in my hotel room and flick through the
two-hundred channels available on US TV."

"Great. I'll send a car to pick you up from your hotel at
seven. See you later. I look forward to hearing this story. It
sounds fascinating."

Chapter One

My slow progress through the roped off zig-zag towards passport control at Kai Tak Airport did not concern me at all. In fact, it made me enormously happy. It meant that I had longer to prepare myself for the typhoon-strength tirade that was about to explode from my mother's mouth the moment that I emerged from those frosted glass doors into the Arrivals hall.

Greeting me with a robust chastisement had become almost customary for my mother. An hour in the queue had given me the chance to add several more witty reposts to my repertoire. I knew almost everything that my mother would say. She might not find my responses amusing, but I would certainly enjoy the game. I might even commit the sin of laughing at my own jokes. This would infuriate my mother further, but I could take it. My sister, Kirsty, would be smirking behind Mum's back, always ready to switch to a serious face should her amusement be in danger of discovery.

It was ridiculous that she should allow herself to get so wound up about my temporary disappearances. After all, I had been running away on a regular basis since my parents had first split up when I was six years old. It was all their fault. They were such idiots when it came to personal relationships and particularly with regards to the wishes of their kids: Kirsty and me.

When Mum suddenly left Dad, when I was six and Kirsty was only four, she had taken all the possessions that she could squeeze into two suitcases, and moved us to a flat about a mile down the road from our nice big Sheffield house. I was already in my second school, Hunter's Bar, and I was very soon to be moved to my third, Psalter Lane, about half a mile up the road. My sister was far too young to start school but she spent all her time crying anyway.

She eventually told me why she was so upset. She was missing her bike. I promised to get it back for her and I was determined to get mine back too. They were both still in the garage at Dad's house.

I needed some help. My best friend, Andy, came with me after school. Dad was at work, so it was easy for us to sneak in and grab the bikes. We ran across the road to the park with them, and then we panicked at the thought that we might get caught. We hid them behind a wall and buried them under some branches and leaves.

Over the next few days, we planned how we might retrieve them. We built a den in the park to hide in, and stocked it up with cans of beans and suchlike from our larders so that we could survive if we had to camp overnight.

The day came, and we went to our den after school to hide until nobody was about. We fell asleep. In the evening, we could hear people calling our names, but that made us more determined to hide. We were scared. In the end, we managed to evade capture for two nights and into a third day. When we saw the police wading through the pond below us, prodding with long sticks, we realised that the situation had become far too serious and we emerged from the woods.

Of course, our parents were overjoyed to see us. That was until after the police had left the scene. At that point, it was over the knee and sore bottoms and tears for both of us! But at least we got our bikes back.

That was all in the past. Since then, I'd run away many times, whenever the opportunity had presented itself. The best times had been during my teen years, so far anyway, when I'd been put on a plane in London with Kirsty to fly out to spend our holidays with Mum. I'd got it down to a fine art. Before boarding the plane, I'd get myself twenty US dollars from the Bureau de Change and tuck it into my passport, which I would keep in my jacket pocket for future use.

My sister hated flying. She would take two Valium and sleep until the plane arrived in Singapore or Hong Kong. At that point, she'd find the note that I'd left on my seat beside her: "Tell Mum that I'll be on the plane twenty-four hours behind this one."

I would choose one of the three or four stopping points along the route and go exploring. It was very simple to walk off the plane at my chosen airport and find the taxi rank. I'd just wave my twenty dollars at a taxi driver and ask, "How much, downtown?"

Whatever they said, I'd offer them half and eventually we'd agree on a fee. When I got to the city centre, I'd save enough cash for the journey back to the airport and wander around for almost twenty-four hours. I learned far more outside school than I ever learned in the classroom. The huge variety of cultures, languages and cuisines that colour the surface of our planet has never ceased to fascinate me.

By jumping off aeroplanes, I had been able to explore Frankfurt, Rome, Tel Aviv, Abu Dhabi, Bombay, New Delhi and many other major cities. On this trip, I'd jumped off the plane in Bangkok and gained what had probably been the biggest lesson of my life so far. Indeed, I could honestly say that the experience had been life-changing.

At last, I managed to get through passport control and pick up my suitcase. Steeling myself, I headed through the exit and into the arrivals hall. Immediately, I spotted Kirsty and Mum waving joyously at me. I made my way over to them and I gave Mum a big hug.

"Where the Hell have you been, Calum?"

"Exploring Bangkok Mum. It was really worthwhile. I'll tell you about it in the taxi home."

"Don't give me 'worthwhile!'" she almost screamed. "You PROMISED me that you would never do this again. I've been worried sick."

"I promised you that I would never hop off the 'plane again in Bombay, Mum. It was Bangkok this time."

"Don't be so insolent and devious. That promise was made for anywhere."

"I wouldn't be stupid enough to make a promise for everywhere, Mum. You wouldn't want to restrict my worldly education, would you?"

"Yes. I damn well would! Donald, I mean Dad, pays for your ticket and he'll have to pay extra now."

We walked out of the terminal and towards the line of taxis.

"He doesn't have to pay any extra. He didn't last time, and he won't this time. I've fixed it. Anyway, it would be too expensive. I had to fly first class on the last leg."

"What?! How did you manage that?"

"It's my technique, perfected over many years. All I do is rock up to the BOAC desk and pretend that I am about to burst into tears. You know: wobble my bottom lip and my voice and tell them that I went outside the airport yesterday and got lost. I say that I don't know what happened. They usually greet me with open arms and tell me that my name must be Calum, which I already know." I laugh.

Mum was horrified by may account of my "outrageous" behaviour. "I don't believe that I am hearing this from my own son. I've brought you up to be better than that. You're just like your father."

"Gosh! Thanks Mum."

"It wasn't meant as a compliment."

"Anyway, the BOAC lady was very happy that I'd turned up and told me that she'd call you to let you know immediately and that there'd be a seat for me on the next flight to Hong Kong. When she came back from the 'phone, she told me that she was sorry but there were no seats available in economy and I'd have to go into first class. I tried to look sad as I assured her that I would just have to grin and bear it and told her that I would never call BOAC 'Better On A Camel' again!"

"You really must be the cheekiest boy on the planet, Calum. At least you're here now. Come on."

The taxi driver put my suitcase in the boot as we instructed him to head for the Star Ferry. Mum didn't like going through the new tunnel which had been opened the previous year. Every time I mentioned it, she reminded me how our rich, rug-collecting friend, Aalim, had crashed his Porsche in the tunnel the first night that it was open, and had been the second person to crash in there the following night. That story had been very amusing at the time, but was now becoming boring.

Once we were driving through the streets of Kowloon, I tried to tell Mum about my experiences in Bangkok. She told me that she'd love to hear about it but that she had more important things to tell me.

"While you've been finishing off your 'A' levels, I've been busy here. Do you remember Margaret Sutherland-White?"

"Yes. Of course. She's an insufferable snob, but absolutely hilarious."

"That's enough of that, darling. I agree that she is a snob, but she has a heart of gold, and we wouldn't have been able to get the Day Centre off the ground without her influence."

"Day Centre? What Day Centre?"

"There's an orphanage in North Point that caters just for physically and mentally handicapped children. All they do, all day, is sleep, eat and perform their natural bodily functions. They have no prospects in life. Mrs Sutherland-White and I decided to do something about it. We've started up a Day Centre for them under the church in Wanchai."

"What happens there?"

"The orphanage have a minibus and they use it to bring the children to the Day Centre at about ten o'clock every weekday. Margaret and I, and a few volunteers, entertain them for a few hours and put them back on the bus. You'll see when we get there."

"What do you mean? I have to get home and get changed. James is expecting me down at the Football Club. We've got plans for this evening."

By this time, we'd arrived at the Star Ferry and Mum paid the driver. I always enjoyed the short trip across the harbour and seeing the 'No Spitting' signs on board made me feel strangely at home. I was wondering what I could do to get out of this situation.

In the few minutes that the taxi took to get from the ferry pier to the church, I tried everything from, "I'm so tired Mum. I haven't slept for forty-eight hours" to "That airline food has made me feel really sick."

Nothing washed with Mum. It seemed that it was all my fault. I had no choice. Helping out at the Day Centre was my only option.

Chapter Two

When we arrived, Margaret emerged from the chaotic noise of kids everywhere to greet me in her sickeningly, elongated tones.

"Ca-a-a-lum! How ma-a-a-rvelous to see you! You've been ve-e-ry na-a-ughty. Again! Giving your poor mother the run-around. Anyway, you are here to help us now. Thank you for coming."

"Hello Mrs Sutherland-White. Nice to see you too. What can I do?"

"Well you could do some painting with those three over there."

I sat down at the table with the three children that Mrs Sutherland-White had indicated to me.

Immediately, I realised that none of them were very well coordinated. Nor could they speak properly: neither Cantonese nor English. They mostly made grunting noises and waved their arms around wildly. But what struck me was that they could communicate their needs with me somehow. They could point, in a fashion, and their facial expressions talked to me.

One little boy was dribbling continuously. He wore a towel around his neck like a bib. I used it to wipe around his face.

Mum came across to me and pointed to some baskets over by the door.

"You'll find clean cloths over there, and there is a basket for used cloths and for soiled clothes. Occasionally we have an accident and you might have to take them to the loo to clean them up. We've got plenty of clean clothes which have been kindly donated by the church congregation, all sizes, so you can dress them and put the dirty clothes in the basket. Margaret's amah washes them all overnight. She's wonderful."

The thought of having to clean up smelly accidents revolted me at first, but I thought that I'd soon get used to it. Parents changed their children's nappies all the time. It couldn't be too much different.

Within minutes, I was really enjoying myself with the children. Even though they were uncoordinated and couldn't speak very well, they were having such great fun. We made a wonderful mess with the paints and the paper. Almost as much paint went on our clothes and the table as went on the paper. I helped them dip their brushes, and even their hands, into the paints and guided them towards the paper. It set me thinking that what they were producing could probably have sold for a fortune in Paris or London, posing as "art nouveau". It certainly looked better than some of the rubbish that I'd seen in galleries. Then again, perhaps not.

Remembering my recent experience Bangkok prompted me to make a vow to myself that I would do all that I could to help these children. They deserved all that we could possibly give to them.

About three o'clock, the orphanage's minibus turned up to take them all home. We helped the driver to get them into their seats and there was much waving and shouting as the bus departed.

I felt suddenly weary and was pleased to be finally heading up Stubbs Road towards our flat. I needed a rest. James would have to wait until tomorrow. I'd call the Football Club and let him know. He would understand.

When we got indoors, Mum offered me some late lunch, but I just had a cup of jasmine tea and went straight to my bedroom. As soon as I lay on my bed, I was asleep.

* * * * *

When I awoke, it was dark outside. The air-conditioning was going full blast in my bedroom. Not only was it noisy, but it was blooming freezing.

I went into a mini panic. What time was it? I looked at my radio alarm clock. 7:20. Dad would be home.

I jumped off my bed and rushed through to greet him.

At eighteen years old, I was already six feet tall, but Dad was another two inches bigger than me. In his day, he had played rugby for the Fiji President's XV, so a bear hug from him was almost how I imagined it might be from a real bear.

"Calum!" he exclaimed, his big white grin shining through the bush of his dark beard. "Welcome home! Grab a beer from the fridge."

He already had a bottle of San Miguel and a glass on the little table beside his chair. He was too civilised to drink straight from the bottle like his slob of a step-son. At least that would be the way Mum would see it. I knew that Don wouldn't even think that way.

Nor would he really care too much that I had spent an unscheduled twenty-four hours in Bangkok, apart from the fact that he would have borne the brunt of my mother's stress and anger.

"We were going to take you out to Jimmy's Kitchen for supper tonight, but perhaps we can do that tomorrow now. You were obviously tired after your adventures."

Mum harrumphed. "Self-inflicted!"

Kirsty giggled.

I loved going to Jimmy's Kitchen. Dad had been a customer since the early nineteen-fifties and we were always treated with the utmost respect there. The dishes were superb and the wine waiter, whom Dad had known for all of the twenty years that he'd been dining there, was just the most amazing entertainer as well as possessing an encyclopedic knowledge of his drinks.

Despite my disappointment, I knew that Dad was right. The experience would be much better if we could take our time. To rush to get ready and then to arrive around nine o'clock to hurry our meals, would not be enjoyable. Better to leave it until the next evening.

The downside was that James would have to wait for another day before we could get on with our plans. I'd meet him down at the pool in the morning though so we could talk about what we should do.

"So. You've got two full months here. I'm assuming you're going back at the beginning of September. Have you got plans for the next eight weeks?"

"Well, I haven't even told Mum this yet, but the Ben Line don't want me to start college in Plymouth until the beginning of January now. So you've got me here for six months."

Kirsty groaned.

I was pleased that my Dad was excited by the news.

"That's great! There's so much we can do together."

"Yes," Mum chipped in. "I've already shown him the Day Centre. We can get it really well established over the next six months. There's a lot to do, but we're going to need funding. Margaret's got some good ideas, but we're going to have to think of a few more."

"I really want to help. I think what you're doing there is wonderful. And those kids can get so much out of it. Of course, I'll help."

"Good! Let's get down there early tomorrow and make a start."

Despite the fact that I was genuinely happy to be helping Mum with the Day Centre, I realised that my plans to meet up with James in the morning had just been blown apart. When I called him at home to tell him, he was disappointed too.

"Just come down to the Football Club when you're finished with your Mum. I'll be there, by the pool, all day.

You must have missed their club sandwiches while you were in England."

"Yeah. I don't think anyone in England knows what a club sandwich is, James. Perhaps we can start up an import-export business based on that idea."

"That'd be good! See you tomorrow."

When I got back into the sitting room, Dad had put another cold bottle of beer on the table next to my chair and had poured himself another glassful.

"As we're staying in tonight, would you like me to get Wei Koo to knock us up some chao fan?" asked Mum.

"Oh, yes please Mum. I'm starving!"

Li Wei Koo was our amah. She lived in a room behind the kitchen of our flat with her husband, Sammy Bintang, who was Indonesian. They had a sweet little girl, a toddler, called Lizzie. She had a Cantonese name too, but we all called her Lizzie.

Wei Koo was a brilliant cook. In fact, she seemed to be brilliant at everything she did. I sometimes wondered if she was magic like that gorgeous Samantha on the TV programme, *Bewitched.* How I envied Darrin Stephens!

Come to think of it, Wei Koo was quite cute too.

Before I'd started on my third San Mig, we were all sitting around the dining table tucking into our delicious rice and, well, everything that Wei Koo had been able to find in the cupboards to throw into her wok. That was the great thing about her chao fan, no serving was like the last one. Every time she served it, it was different, yet it was always absolutely delicious.

Mum always told me off for liberally splashing soy sauce all over my chao fan. She told me that it was an insult to Wei Koo. But each to their own taste.

I was still very tired, despite my extended afternoon nap. I had a couple more beers and then enjoyed a small glass, "a snifter", of my Dad's top quality single malt before going through to my bedroom. I only managed to read about three pages of Nigel Tranter's *Black Douglas* before I fell asleep.

Chapter Three

The following morning, I was up reasonably early, at about half past seven. Mum did us a fry up as Wei Koo scuttled around tidying up and polishing every exposed piece of wood in sight, including the floor. The flat was always immaculate. Lizzie crawled around after her mother, chasing her like a playful puppy.

The parrots, Chippy and Pedro, were in fine voice, as they always were in the mornings. They were close to the rear balcony in the laundry room and could hear all the jungle birds in the trees on the hill behind our block of flats. They were the best pair of bird impressionists in Hong Kong, so good that some of the smaller jungle birds would come and perch on the wall of the balcony to speak to them.

Occasionally, they would call out some recognisable words in recognisable voices.

"Wei Koo!" they would call in a perfect imitation of Mum's voice.

The amah would come scurrying through to the kitchen.

"Yes Mem."

"It wasn't me, Wei Koo. It was that blooming parrot again."

Wei Koo would go back to her polishing. She always answered Pedro's call. She would be ashamed of herself if she ever failed to respond to her mistress's genuine call.

Dad had already gone off to work. Mum and Kirsty and I only had to stand on the road side for about two minutes before and taxi came down the hill from Won Nai Chung Gap and stopped to pick us up. Less than ten minutes later we pulled up outside the church. The driver of the minibus was already helping Margaret and a couple of other helpers to get the children inside. Two of the children couldn't walk and had to be carried. Most of the others were quite mobile, even though some of them struggled with huge determination. They were all laughing and chattering away.

Once everybody was inside and seated, and those who wanted beakers of water or juice had their needs met, Mum sat down at the piano and began to play random tunes that we all could sing along to. Possibly three or four of the children could sing in tune but the words mattered very little to them. The rest just made a noise. A few of them swayed around in time, or out of time, with Mum's tempo. What really mattered was that they were all enjoying themselves tremendously.

Mum had a flash of inspiration.

Turning to Kirsty and me, she asked, "Do you remember sitting on top of the piano and singing the songs from *Salad Days*?"

We did. We were about the same age as these kids when we used to do that and obviously we'd been much smaller than we were now.

"Come on then. Up you get!"

We looked at each other, both thinking, *Is she crazy?*

Nevertheless, we obeyed, at the risk of looking stupid.

Once we'd launched into *We're Looking for a Piano* and *We Said We Wouldn't Look Back*, the children got even more excited. Those who were able to, got up and started dancing. One little girl, who remained in her chair, bounced up and down waving her arms around. Suddenly, she leaped up in the air and landed on the floor laughing her head off.

One of the helpers stepped forward and put her back on her seat.

When we'd all had enough of the music, we broke up into little groups to play with the scant materials that we had: paper, paints, plasticine, balls, and clothes for dressing up and so on.

Mum explained that the kids all had nicknames. The one that had just jumped out of her seat was called Harriet because, whenever she got really excited, she would bounce up and down, as I had seen, and then jump straight up in the air. She couldn't walk, but she could fly!

"So why is she called Harriet, Mum?"

"After the vertical take-off jet that the RAF use: the Harrier."

I burst out laughing. "That's hilarious. She IS just like a Harrier jump jet when she takes off like that. Very appropriate."

I asked Mum, "Do you usually start the day off with some music?"

"Yes. They love it. Sometimes we put on a little play. Nothing planned. We just make it up as we go along. If they want to join in, we let them. It's good for them. Whatever stimulates their minds. Remember that if they weren't here, all they'd be doing would be sitting around in their cots at the orphanage."

"How terrible for them. Your Day Centre is wonderful Mum." I thought a bit more about what I'd said. "Don't you think that it could be even better if we had more toys and equipment though?"

"You're right. But we rely entirely on charity; mostly what the members of the church and their families bring in for us."

After we'd had a bit of a break, we continued to play with the children until Margaret told us that the sandwiches were ready. We distributed the food and drink. Most of the children could feed themselves and drink from beakers. Four of them needed some help with the sandwiches and drank from Tommee Tippee mugs.

After lunch, the minibus came back and we helped the driver to get the children back on board, waving to them as they departed.

It didn't take long to tidy up. Kirsty and I told Mum that we'd see her later and headed back down Queen's Road towards the Football Club and the race track.

All our old friends were sitting around the pool. There was much screaming and hugging and kissing. More drinks were ordered: beers and lemonade and limes. I finally got my chops around my long-awaited club sandwich. Delicious!

After lunch, I got my trunks on and made a few pathetic attempts at somersaults off the springboard. Most of the time I landed flat on my back. It stung. It really hurt. Everybody laughed.

"The perfect reverse belly flop, Calum. Welcome back!"

Of course, James and Helmut spun and entered the water with hardly a splash. We were all showing off in front of the girls. My theory was that they were more impressed by my comedy spins than by any Olympic athletes. My friends stuck to their converse theory. I never really understood who was correct, and no girl was ever going to tell me.

After a while, James and I were able to break away for a private chat.

"I've got stacks of business cards from Chen Wong. We can write a few out now so that we're ready for tonight."

"I'm fine to write on the backs of a load of cards now James, but I have to go out with my family tonight. Jimmy's Kitchen. We'll have to get on with our business tomorrow night."

"That's OK Calum. Hennessy Road's going to be crawling tomorrow night anyway. There are two US ships due in tomorrow morning. All the clubs will be packed."

We walked round to the veranda by the bowling green and found a quiet table where we could get on with writing our names on the backs of the business cards that Chen Wong had supplied.

This was our best money-making scam. Chen Wong owned the Spitting Cobra nightclub on Hennessy Road in Wanchai. James and I would patrol the other clubs in the street and the surrounding streets and give out cards to unsuspecting American and Australian soldiers and sailors who were in Hong Kong on their rest and recuperation leave from the Vietnam War. They all carried thick bundles of bank notes in their pockets and all they wanted to do was to enjoy spending as much of their cash as possible.

Our message was very simple, and the servicemen were very grateful.

"Just head on down to the Spitting Cobra. Present this card with my name on the back to the doorman, and he'll let you in for free. You'll get your first drink free. Anything you want. There's always live music and there are plenty of lovely girls. Have fun!"

The usual response was "Wow! Thanks man."

"See you down there a bit later."

James and I held the view that we were providing a public service by helping them in their quest to spend and enjoy. Before they'd come ashore, they had all been paid at least three month's salary in a single pay packet. They'd had nothing to spend their money on in the war zone, so they were absolutely loaded. And they really DID want to spend it all. They realised that next week they would be going back to Vietnam and that they may not even survive their next tour. Maximise the fun was their principal objective. And why not?

By the time we went back to the pool to join the others, we'd written well over two hundred cards each. That would keep us going for a few days.

After another hour of pure fun with our friends, Kirsty and I made our way back up the hill through the cemetery to our flat on Stubbs Road. On the way, we paused to watch a praying mantis in a tree. It had caught a cricket and was steadily devouring it. They're such amazing looking beasts, almost like alien beings from Doctor Who.

* * * * *

Walking into Jimmy's Kitchen in Theatre Lane in Central was like coming home all over again. The place was full of familiar sights and sounds and people. The atmosphere always filled me with happiness and joy. Apart from that, I was certain that I was about to eat the best cuisine available in the whole of Hong Kong, and that was really saying something.

The boss himself came out to greet Dad as if he was his long lost brother. They had known each other for more than two decades. Then he made a big fuss of the rest of us.

Mum, Dad and Kirsty were served glasses of Kir Royale. I tried to be Mister Sophisticate and went for a Lemon Gingerini. Typically, George, the long established wine waiter knew exactly what I was after and mixed it to perfection.

Dad knew precisely what I would like as my starter, even though my favourite in any restaurant was usually whitebait. He asked the waiter if the oysters were fresh. On being assured that they had been flown in from Australia that very morning, he ordered a dozen Oysters Kirkpatrick to share between the two of us. This dish, served at Jimmy's Kitchen, would be difficult to beat as a starter. Kirsty and Mum didn't like the thought of "slimy" oysters though, so they chose alternatives.

As expected, none of us were disappointed. I could easily have eaten another half dozen oysters, but it seemed like a good idea to leave some room for the delights to come.

When the main course arrived, I stared at my beautifully presented pepper steak and I knew that it would be as good as it looked. The aromas that filled my nostrils set my oral juices running in no time. Nevertheless, I hesitated. I was finding it very difficult to bring myself to serve up my vegetables from the hot dishes that had been laid in the centre of table. I could feel tears welling up into my eyes. The memories of my short visit to Bangkok were threatening to spoil my dinner. I started to cry.

As I'd wandered around that city, almost aimlessly, I had come to a splendid palace. It was adorned with a dazzling golden roof. The palace was huge. I wondered who could possibly live inside such a magnificent building. The sparkling roof dazzled me. I heard some people, who were standing close to me, speaking English. I remarked that the roof actually looked as if it were made of gold.

"That's because it really IS made of gold!"

"Really? It is made of real gold?"

"Well, not entirely. Most of it is painted gold. But there are tiles of real gold embedded in the roof to make it sparkle like that."

I couldn't believe such extravagance.

To make matters worse for me, I noticed that, against the walls of the palace there were sheets of corrugated iron under which families were living in their own dirt and squalor. Large families sat around in the shade of the sheets of metal. Some children played in the street. The whole place stank like an open sewer.

I sat down on the ground on the opposite side of the road and took in the view before me. My eyes flicked from the poor families to the extravagant architecture of the golden palace. The huge contrast between the rich and the poor struck me hard, as never before.

I wept. I sat and I wept for a whole two hours. What I was observing was utterly obscene. I decided that I had to do something about it.

The taxi driver who had brought me from the airport had tried to charge me four dollars for the trip. I had persuaded him to take me for just two dollars. That left me eighteen. I thought I'd better save myself four dollars for the journey back to the airport, just in case I couldn't negotiate a better price. That left me with fourteen dollars to spend on myself.

I walked down the street to a market that I'd passed on my walk up to the palace. I found a stall with a large selection of vegetables and asked the stall-holder to pack some bags with as many goods as she would give me for fourteen US dollars. It was much more than I could carry on my own. She mustered three young boys to help me carry the bags back to the palace. I was sorry that I had no coins left to give them a tip. I gave them a packet of chewing gum that I just happened to have in my pocket.

The families were delighted with the food that we took them. They made me stay so that I could drink some of their revolting tea with them. I didn't understand a word that they were saying, apart from "kob kun krab" which I had learned meant "thank you." They directed plenty of smiles in my direction. From time to time, I burst into tears. These poor people. I knew full well that the relief that I had brought them was only temporary. I just wished that I could have done more for them.

This was an event that was to change my life.

As I made my way back to the airport in a two dollar taxi, later that day, I still felt very emotional. How could those very rich people live with such poverty on their doorstep? Had they no social conscience? Were they blind? Had they no feelings?

As usual, I made my way to the BOAC desk and carried out my well-practiced feeling-sorry-for-myself routine. It worked a treat and I was soon on board the flight to Hong Kong with the bonus prize of being seated in first class.

On the home-bound flight, I had plenty of time to reflect on my experience. Those wretched families who were living in squalor in the shadows of that great, golden palace, were happy with what they had. They celebrated when I presented them with a few bags of food. They smiled and offered me hospitality.

Had I gone to the gates of the palace, bearing small gifts, would they have invited me in for a cup of tea? I think not.

By the time we landed at Kai Tak, marvelling at the sight of the blocks of the blocks of flats towering above us on both sides as we came down, I had formed my life motto in my mind.

"One world, one people, care for them all."

That evening, at Jimmy's kitchen, I was already feeling that I was betraying my motto. There I was, about to tuck into a delicious pepper steak, while there were families living in the streets of Central, within a few hundred yards of me where I was sitting, who would have to scrape around for their one scant meal per day. My appetite had gone.

Mum broke into my reverie.

"Are you alright, darling? You look a bit pale. Are you crying? What's wrong?"

"Yes Mum. I'm OK thanks. I just don't feel so hungry now."

"Then you definitely ARE ill! I have never known you do anything other than clear your plate in this restaurant."

As I finally got around to spooning a few vegetables onto my plate I told her, "I was just thinking of something I saw in Bangkok. I need to tell you about it. It's important."

"Well you will go running off and worrying us all to death. It's your fault if you saw something disgusting is putting you off your food."

"It's not like that Mum. You'll understand when I tell you."

I was right. By the time we'd finished our main course, she did understand. I had managed to tell my family the whole story between mouthfuls. My appetite had returned. Mum rather surprised me when she heaped praise on me for my actions. That didn't happen very often. Dad and Kirsty were also full of praise.

"You can be a really lovely boy sometimes, Calum," said my sister, as if she was shocked by the thought. "Very rarely though," she added.

I enjoyed the praise, and my appetite suddenly returned as soon as the first mouthful of steak entered my mouth. I really didn't want to talk about Bangkok any more. They were making too much of it. Part of me was wishing that I'd never told them.

My plate was clean and I wanted to get on with the dessert: Satellite. I'd never had deep-fried ice cream anywhere other than Jimmy's Kitchen. And flaming brandy over the top of it made this most amazing dish into something even more special. Kirsty went for her usual, Baked Alaska, which was always quite spectacular as they would shape it into a boat or a plane especially for her. They liked to spoil us.

The highlight of any trip to Jimmy's Kitchen was when George came to the table to serve Dad's after-dinner Armagnac. He would pour a finger of brandy straight from the bottle with unerring, well-practised accuracy. To prove it, he would lay the brandy glass on its side on the table and gently roll it. The liquid would reach the lip of the glass exactly. Not a drop would spill and it would be impossible to add a single drop without a spillage.

Once he'd demonstrated his expertise, George would stand Dad's glass upright and "accidentally" tip the bottle to double the measure.

"Oops! Slipped again, Sir," he would chuckle. Every time, the same. But always, we would all laugh at his little joke.

As ever, our family dinner was an absolute pleasure, but I couldn't avoid being haunted by the contrasting images of the rich and the poor in Bangkok that were surely burned into my memory forever.

Chapter Four

The next day, I made my excuses to Mum and told her that I was heading straight down to the pool to meet James. She wasn't at all happy and told me to come to the Day Centre once I'd met with my friend. I promised that I would, but I didn't know how long I would be. Kirsty went with Mum and asked me to tell the girls that she'd be there by lunchtime.

When I got to the club Helmut, Iona and Karen were all waiting for me. I couldn't see James anywhere.

"Hi Calum. Where's Kirsty today?" asked Karen.

"She's gone with Mum to the Day Centre. She said she'd be down later when she's finished there."

"What is this Day Centre all about?" queried Helmut.

"Well, Mum and Margaret Suther...." I started to explain.

"It's a brilliant idea!" interrupted Iona. "Kirsty's Mum and her friend found out about these poor handicapped kids in an orphanage. They're literally locked in there all day with nothing to do. They started the Day Centre to give the kids a better life." She went on to explain the place much better than I ever could.

I was distracted as I wondered where James had got to. He'd promised to be here to discuss our plans.

"Has anybody seen James?"

"Yes. He went off to play squash with Len."

"Who the fuck is Len?"

"Oh. I forgot you haven't met him yet," Karen said. "He's new here. His Dad got fast-tracked for membership." That explained something. Usually, it took new members at least six months as guests before they passed all the various committees and were accepted into full membership. "I suppose it's because of his position. Commander Millward,

Len's Dad, is the new Commissioner of Prisons. Anyway, Len seems really nice, and James says he's very good at squash. He's definitely a great swimmer and diver. Great body too!"

Iona giggled. I felt a pang of jealousy. In my opinion, if anyone around here had a great body, it was Iona.

"AND he can beat your somersaults off the board, Calum."

"Well that's not too difficult, Karen. Even Iona can do that better than Calum," laughed Helmut.

"Okay. Okay. But at least I entertain you all with my pathetic attempts."

"Yes. There's no disputing that."

I disliked Helmut sometimes. Especially when he showed me up in front of Iona.

Iona was totally gorgeous and such great fun. She was always up for a laugh. Although she was Kirsty's best friend and the same age as my sister, I'd always fancied her and she knew it. She deliberately flounced around in front of me in that tiny purple bikini.

I was happy to see James finally appear accompanied by a tall, wiry, blond boy who was grinning from ear to ear. It had to be Len.

"Hi. You must be Calum. Nice to meet you. I've heard such a lot about you. Is it true that you're a naval officer?"

"Well, I was at a naval school until a couple of weeks ago. I'm waiting to start my training to be a marine engineering officer in the Merchant Navy."

"Wow! We'll have to have a chat about that sometime."

"Why? Do you have a special interest in the navy?"

"Yes. All things maritime really. And engineering too. Dad wants me to join the Hong Kong police, but what I'd really like to do is to go into the Royal Navy or the Merchant Navy, just like you."

"Well, it meant that I studied some unusual subjects at school, such as marine science, seamanship and navigation."

"Gosh. I really do envy you. I'd have loved to have taken those subjects at my school."

"I only studied them up to 'O' level though. I took more conventional 'A' levels: pure maths, applied maths, physics and chemistry."

"A sailor and a scientist. I'm truly honoured to meet you, Calum."

I was beginning to get a bit embarrassed by his enthusiasm. He didn't know the real me yet. I was sure that he'd be disappointed.

My thoughts turned to James. Hoping that he'd be worn out and I could take advantage, I challenged him to a game of squash.

"Definitely Calum. Len beat me, so I could do with a victory to even up my day."

"Don't be cheeky James. We'll see."

"Just give me a few minutes to have a drink and cool down. Both courts are free, so we'll be alright to go straight on. Actually, I might have a quick swim. You coming?"

Without waiting for an answer, he dived into the pool. I followed him.

Once we were far enough away from the crowd, James spoke quietly to me.

"Be careful what you say about what we do, Calum. I am not sure how much we can trust Len yet. I think he's up for a bit of fun, but if he gets a sniff of some of the borderline illegal stuff we do, the bad stuff, we could find ourselves in trouble."

"Thanks for the warning. He seems like a nice chap though."

"Oh yeah. He's nice enough. But if he let slip something to his Dad or any of his Dad's police chums...."

"I get you. Don't worry. Anyway, are we heading down Hennessy Road tonight?"

"Of course! I'm skint. We need to make some serious cash."

"We will. I've got a good feeling about tonight. Now, how about that game of squash?"

"Ten minutes to get a drink, and I'll be right with you. Do you want one?"

"No thanks. You can buy me a beer when I've wiped you off the court."

He laughed as he climbed out of the shallow end and headed for the pool bar.

"That'll be the day!" he called back over his shoulder.

* * * * *

We just played best of three, and James beat me 10-8 in the deciding game. It was always close between us. We showered and returned to the pool-side to join the others. I bought James a beer, or rather I signed it off on Dad's tab, and then I made my excuses and left.

I was beginning to feel guilty that I had let Mum and the kids down. I needed to set my mind at rest by going up to the Day Centre for the last couple of hours.

When I got there, it was absolute chaos. Only Mum, Margaret, Kirsty and Heather, a quiet lady from the church, were looking after all of the children. There was equipment and paint and plasticine and toys all over the place. The kids were running riot.

My guilt deepened.

Mum was emerging from the toilets supporting a little girl who couldn't walk on her own. I caught up with her just as she found a convenient seat in which to rest the girl.

"I'm really sorry Mum." And I was. "I didn't realise that you'd be so short-handed or I would have come down with you straight after breakfast. Is it often like this?"

"I didn't expect to be short either. But you're here now. Perhaps you can help Heather and Kirsty to tidy up? Then we might put on a little play for them."

It didn't take very long to restore some order to the room. Mopping the paint off floor could wait until after the bus had taken them all back to the orphanage.

We arranged the seats in a semi-circle and then started to improvise a play.

Mum encouraged me to show them the drill routines that I'd learnt at naval school. I marched up and down, shouting orders to myself, turning left and right and about, and halting and saluting. They absolutely loved it, cheering and clapping and making quite a din. Kirsty joined in, marching behind me and mimicking my movements as best she could. That inspired some of the more mobile children to join in too.

Margaret and Heather handed out our makeshift percussion instruments: tin cans and rattles and the like, to those who were still seated, so that they could be the military band.

Everybody in the room was having such fun. There was an abundance of laughter. We were all so happy. Harriet did her usual trick, flying up into the air and crash-landing, SMACK, on the floor. It must have hurt her, but she was laughing her head off as Heather picked her up and put her back in her seat. Within two minutes she was back on the floor again.

A little boy whom I had hardly noticed the previous day, became very animated indeed. He climbed onto a box and started barking nonsensical commands at the top of his voice and saluting us every time we went past.

Mum shouted at him. "Fai Cheung! Get down! You'll fall and hurt yourself!"

He totally ignored her.

"What's his name, Mum?"

"Cheung. He can be a damned nuisance sometimes," she answered above the din.

I warmed to him immediately. She often said the same about me when she wasn't calling me "a pain in the arse."

I marched up and halted in front of him. I saluted.

"Parade present and correct and ready for your inspection, General Cheung, Sah!" I reported in a very serious tone.

I could see that he was delighted. He swung me a huge, expansive salute and promptly fell off his box.

Mum squealed and rushed forward to pick him up.

All of the children burst into hysterics. General Cheung jumped back up onto his box and joined their hilarity. Mum's sigh of relief was audible, even above all the noise that surrounded her.

The atmosphere was wonderful.

I told Mum that I had an idea for the next day.

"I'll bring my naval cap down and put it on Cheung's head. We'll stage a march past, and he can take the salute."

"He'll love that. And all the children will too."

We were so involved in the activities that we hadn't noticed the time. The minibus driver was standing in the doorway watching us. He was laughing too.

The children didn't want to leave, but we managed to get them all onto the bus eventually. Most of them understood that they'd be coming back for more fun the following day.

Chapter Five

As arranged, I met James at the bar in the Spitting Cobra on Hennessy Road just before seven o'clock. There were less than ten people in the whole place, and it was very quiet. That was until Chen Wong came bursting out of his office. Spreading his arms wide, the immaculately dressed, portly little man advanced towards us with a broad grin splitting his face. As usual, his dark hair was slicked down with Brylcreem. The smell almost put me off my beer.

"James! Calum! My friends! How good to see you both!"

"A pleasure to see you too, Chen Wong."

"Colin," Chen Wong addressed the barman, whom I had never seen before, "drinks for these two gentlemen, Mister King and Mister McDougal, are always on the house. They don't pay for anything in my club. Understood?"

"Yes Mister Wong. Welcome Mister King. Welcome Mister McDougal." He nodded to each of us in turn. "May I get you another drink?"

"No thanks, Colin. We're fine," I responded.

The poor chap seemed very nervous. There was no need to be. We were only teenagers, but I suppose that we were Chen Wong's guests, and he was the 'Mister Big' in this place.

"Are you going to be working the clubs for me tonight?"

"That's what we're here for," said James. "We'll fill your club. We need the money. We'll get busy as soon as we've finished this beer."

"Good. See you back here in a couple of hours. And it'll be the usual twenty dollars for every card with your name on when we count them on Friday."

Minutes later we were in The Silver Spoon approaching American and Australian servicemen, many of whom were already well-oiled. As expected, they were enormously grateful for the promise of free entry and a first free drink when they presented our cards at the door of the Spitting Cobra. We told them that we'd catch up with them later and moved on to the Ivory Moon.

By just after nine, we'd repeated the operation in all the clubs up and down Hennessy Road and Wanchai Road where we were able to get in without being recognised. A few of the clubs knew what we were up to, and we were barred. There were a few exceptions to that rule. Although we were well known at the Playgirl, the 747 and the Pussycat, we still would be let in, because the management knew that we'd bring custom back their way later in the evening. By the time we'd done our rounds and returned to the Spitting Cobra, it was packed to capacity. We were inundated with offers of drinks, and we accepted many of those offers.

"Hey Calum. What're you havin' buddy?"

"Just a vodka and lemonade for me, please."

Of course, Colin and the rest of the bar staff knew to serve us just glasses of lemonade and charge the punters around twenty dollars for the privilege.

Then it was on to the next phase of the operation. Pointing to the line of girls at the bar, I would ask the unsuspecting soldiers and sailors if they liked any of them.

"Yeah man! That gal second from the end on the left is some hot candy. Do you know her?"

"Yes. Of course. I know all of the girls. That one's name is Michelle. She drinks Bacardi and Coke. Just give her my card," I'd tell him handing over another card, "and tell her that Calum sent you across."

"Gee, thanks Calum, You're the man!"

Off he'd go to spend twenty or thirty dollars on a plain Coke for the girl and the same for whatever drink he was having. Quite often, they would fall for the ruse of the girl asking for Champagne. At two-hundred dollars a bottle, it was some very expensive fizzy plonk.

They might even go further: upstairs to one of the many small bedrooms above the club for some fun and a smoke, or more. They'd spend a fortune, but they'd get maximum enjoyment out of the night before returning to their ships.

James and I worked very hard all evening, but we also had a lot of fun and we knew that we'd reap our rewards on Friday. It was only Wednesday, so we knew that we could double our money the following night.

We had another beer, then moved on to our local, The Godown. Some nights were really lively, especially Thursday evening when there was always live jazz. That was my favourite evening at the Godown. The bands all knew Mum very well and would often entice her up to jam with them on the piano. Her concert pianist days were long forgotten and improvisation and trad jazz were much more her style these days.

Tonight, there were only half a dozen customers in the bar. We knew them all. It was nice to be able to relax and chat with them until gone midnight. Unfortunately, a loud American sailor invaded our tranquillity.

"Wow! This really is a British bar, ain't it?"

"Yes. It certainly is," replied James. "But you are most welcome to join us. Come and sit down."

"Are you British?" he addressed James directly. You look more like a damned Chink to me fella. Where are you from?"

James swore at him in Cantonese before politely replying that he had been born and brought up in Hong Kong. "My mother is Cantonese and my father is English.

He came here to work in 1950, and he's stayed here ever since. Hong Kong is our home."

"Guess you're as British as the rest of the guys in this dump then. Couldn't stand it myself. Never been in such a quiet bar in my life."

"Do you like jazz?" I asked.

"Yeah. 'Course. Jazz was born in the States. That's where you find real jazz."

"You should come here tomorrow night then. It'll be packed, so get here early. I'm sure that you'll enjoy it. Great food and live trad jazz all night."

"Sounds good. I might just come along. Won't be as good as back home in the States though."

This chap was really beginning to get on my nerves, but I was determined to keep my cool. Maybe we could play a game with him and put him in his place.

"My name's Calum. This is James."

He held out his hand to each of us in turn.

"Hey Calum! Hey James! Pleased to meet you. My name is Hank." Somehow, I knew it would be something like that. *Hank the Wank,* was what immediately came into my mind.

"Nice to meet you too Wah...." Oops! "... Hank. You should definitely come down here tomorrow night. Bring a few friends."

"I'll probably come along on my own. Most of my so-called friends are dull and boring."

I suspected that this little creep had no friends at all. I could understand why. He had managed to wind both of us up within one minute of meeting us.

Although Hank was short, probably about five-foot-eight, it was obvious that his tight t-shirt was packed with muscles. He looked as if he spent a great deal of his life on board USS Whatever-ship-he-came-in-on pumping iron. He was probably only two or three years older than us. I'd put him at twenty or twenty-one.

As the evening wore on, Hank continued to bore us with stories of how much better and bigger everything was "back home than in either *Great* Britain or in Hong Kong." He sarcastically emphasised the word "Great".

"*Why,* you even have the neck to call these buildings around here *SKY* scrapers! You should see my fine home town of Chicago. When I left home for this tour they were just capping off the tallest building in the world."

We were so unimpressed with that news that we fell silent.

"I can tell you're impressed," he said. "You heard me right. The tallest building in the world. It has over one hundred floors."

"You're right, Hank," I replied. "The tallest building in Hong Kong is about to be opened in the next couple of weeks. You may have seen it in the daylight down by the waterfront. The white one with all the big, round windows. It's called the Connaught Centre and it only has half that number of floors. But it certainly beats your tallest building in the world in one way."

"Oh yeah? How?"

"Well, the locals call it 'The House of the Thousand Arseholes'. I'll bet your tower doesn't have that many arseholes."

James laughed loudly.

Hank laughed loudly too. "See! That just about sums this town up. It's full of ass-holes! Ha ha ha!"

I had to join in the laughter.

Getting serious once more, he asked us about the jazz stars that might perform here on Thursday night.

"It's usually local bands that you'll never have heard of in Chicago, but we have had the likes of Acker Bilk, Chris Barber and Kenny Ball playing here."

"Never heard of any of those guys," Hank said. This time I really was genuinely shocked. I thought of all three of them as world famous.

"Really? Who have you heard of then?"

"In Chicago we might see Chet Baker or Dizzy Gillespie," he rattled back at me quite casually.

This news blew my mind, but I tried to keep a dead pan face. That was fantastic. I envied him.

"So, have you actually seen them perform?" I asked.

He hesitated. "Not actually in the flesh, but I could have if I'd wanted to. They're always in town. It's just that I have too much action going on in my own life. Chicago never stops buzzin', you know."

"I can imagine," said James. "Do you want another beer, Hank?"

"No thanks. But I'll have a double Bourbon on the rocks if you're buyin'"

"OK. San Mig for you Calum?"

"Yes please, James."

While James was at the bar fetching the drinks, Hank asked me, "Is that all you guys ever drink. That pissy local beer? Don't you ever hit the liquor?"

"Yes. We do sometimes, but today's been a long day. We're just relaxing with a few San Miguels."

"So, what's your tipple, Calum?"

"My favourite is a single malt. Neat. James likes to drink dark rum. Sometimes with peppermint cordial."

"Sounds gross! The rum with peppermint, I mean. Don't mind the single malt though."

"Each to their own tastes, Hank."

We waited in silence till James returned with our drinks.

Hank thanked James, toasted us with a "Cheers!", slammed the glass on the table and then knocked his drink back in one. "Whoo! You guys ready for another?"

Stupid question, as our glasses had not yet touched our lips.

"No thanks, Hank," said James. "We'll be getting home after this one. Maybe tomorrow night or Friday?"

"That's the trouble with you Limeys." He looked at James. "Or half-Limey in your case," he laughed. You guys just can't drink. I could drink both of you under the table and still be stone-cold sober."

We looked at each other. It sounded like a challenge. James winked and half smiled.

I looked Hank in the eyes and accepted his challenge, whether he meant it or not. "We'll take you up on that. How long are you here in Hong Kong?"

"Two weeks. Just arrived. And I'm always up for a drinking competition. You'll lose!"

"OK. You're on. Not tomorrow though. We have work to do so we'll be late getting here. We'd need the whole evening. How about Friday?"

"Yeah. Friday. I'll be here at eight to start. What are the rules?"

"We each put our wallets; sorry, pocket-books, in the centre of the table at the beginning of the evening. We run up a tab for all of our drinks. The loser is the first to puke or to pass out. The other two pay for the drinks out of his cash and make sure that he gets safely home."

"Sounds great! That'll be a free night for me then. You guys are dust!"

As we finished our beers, Hank downed another two double Bourbons. The American continued to brag about the size, speed and greatness of everything in his own country compared to ours. His words became slurred. We were convinced that he would be regretting his rash behaviour within a few days, particularly as we would be priming the barman at the Godown to dilute our drinks whilst keeping Hank's at full strength.

When we left, Hank decided to stay on for "just one more."

Chapter Six

By the time I got back to our flat, it was almost one o'clock. I switched on the TV. The best programmes were always on at this time of night. I loved the American detective dramas such as McCloud, who rode a white steed down Broadway like a cowboy in the Big Apple, and my favourite of all: Columbo with Peter Falk as the bumbling, but ever so effective Lieutenant. The latter was so amusing and clever. It was the opposite of a whodunnit, because we knew who did it from the very beginning. It was just a case of how Columbo would catch the perpetrator.

Then there was McMillan and Wife.

All three were good shows.

If it wasn't a detective show, it would be one of the old, black-and-white horror films featuring Count Dracula, Frankenstein's monster or the Lizard Man from the Swamp. I found these hilarious, yet compelling viewing.

Even when I eventually got to bed, I couldn't sleep. Thoughts of the money that James and I could make and how we'd make it, and then the inevitable downfall of Hank, filled my mind. As I drifted off to sleep, these images were replaced by the anticipation of activities in the Day Centre. Despite my rather wicked activities in Wanchai and my intentions towards our new American acquaintance, I was overwhelmed with a desire to help those poor orphan children whose young lives had been dealt the double blow of being both parentless and handicapped. By comparison, I was extremely lucky and privileged. I felt compelled to help them all I could.

* * * * *

I'd hardly closed my eyes, it seemed, when my mother was knocking on my door.

"Darling? Are you awake?"

I groaned.

"I'm going down to the Day Centre in half an hour. I've made you some fresh coffee. If you're coming down with me, you'd better shake a leg now."

I groaned again. I looked at my radio alarm clock.

It was flashing brightly at me: 08:45.

I swung my legs over the side and planted my feet on the floor. The air conditioning was very loud. I wrapped my batik sarong around my waist and headed for the bathroom to wash and shave, taking a diversion into the sitting room to pick up my mug of hot coffee. It smelt great and I was already waking up.

Mum waited for me. Kirsty, of course, had been ready for ages. Chippy and Pedro were busy squawking at the wild birds out the back and occasionally calling out to Wei Koo. They were so naughty but I loved them.

We went down to the basement in the lift and stood on the side of Stubbs Road for only two minutes before a taxi came down the hill from Wong Nai Chung Gap direction and picked us up. In the few minutes that it took us to travel down to the church, Kirsty asked me what was in the large paper bag that I'd brought with me.

I showed her. I had my naval cap and a few pairs of socks.

She collapsed into a giggling fit. Mum turned round and saw what I had. She laughed too.

I explained that the socks were to entertain the kids with sock puppets. I'd seen an American show with a lady called Shari Lewis. It was tremendously entertaining and children could easily copy the fun with just a sock and a little imagination. I enjoyed it myself.

Mum asked me why I'd brought my officer's cap.

I immediately put a sock on my hand and picked up the article in question. With a terrible American accent, made even worse by my rubbish attempt at ventriloquism, I answered her. "Oh my goodness! What is this? Is it a plate? Is it a space ship? Oh no! It's an officer's cap for General Cheung to wear as he inspects the troops and salutes the march past."

"I love that idea, Calum. I can just see them all parading up and down and Fai Cheung standing on his box, full of his own importance."

We arrived and went inside to prepare for the arrival of the multitude. I hid the cap for later use. When they arrived, we got them all sat down and Mum played the piano while we all sang. Harmony was far out of reach, but enjoyment of music is universal and these children became so totally wrapped up in it. I was looking around at them all. I loved them. They were so much happier with the simple entertainment that we were proving than many children I'd seen who were much more "wealthy" and privileged.

My grandmother's definition of wealth popped into my mind.

"Do you know where the word 'wealth' comes from, Calum?" she would often ask me. To humour her, I would always answer that I didn't know. I liked her to tell me.

"It is a combination of 'well-being' and 'good health'. If you have both of those, you are indeed wealthy. It has nothing to do with how much money you have or how many possessions. Without your health, you cannot enjoy such material things. A rich man who is sick and unhappy will never be wealthy."

My grandmother had no money, but she was very wealthy. She was also very wise. I thought that she could have made it all up, but that didn't matter to me. I just loved her explanation.

When some of the children began to get a little restless, Kirsty produced my socks and we put on a short show for them. It was all nonsensical but it had them amused and they all wanted to have a go. It was lucky that I'd brought so many pairs of socks, and even some odd ones. Before long, most of them had at least one puppet and they were all waving them about and making noises. I suppose it meant something to them. We were just happy that THEY were so happy.

It also gave me an excuse to ask Mum for some new socks. After all, we had no other option than to leave the ones that I had brought to the Day Centre when we finished for the day.

After a short break for lunch, consisting drinks and some snacks, followed by the necessary tidying up and toilet breaks, it was time for General Cheung's big parade.

He was delighted with my naval cap, as I knew he would be. In no time at all he had it on his head and was shouting orders at his army, or navy, or unruly squad of whatever personnel he imagined he commanded.

His 'subordinates' were clearly enjoying it as much as he was.

Harriet took off, as usual. Kirsty picked her up and held her hands to support her so that she could march up and down with the rest.

I did the same with a very quiet little girl who I knew could not walk. I'd observed her, sitting contemplating the activities around her. She had been painting the previous day and had joined in with the singing and the glove puppetry. She had a round face, rosy cheeks and a lovely smile. I judged her to be about six or seven years old.

When I tried to march her around the room with the rest of General Cheung's squad, her legs crossed and uncrossed and she bore hardly any weight. But I could feel her determination. I sensed that she really wanted to walk straight and to do so unaided.

Mum turned to Mrs Sutherland-White and rather cruelly said, "Look at that Margaret. Knit one, pearl one, knit one, pearl one. She is knitting!"

We all laughed at her joke.

Perhaps I was even more cruel than my own mother when I suggested, "Maybe that's what we should call her: Knitting."

"Yes. 'Knitting' would be most apt," Mum agreed. And so the name stuck.

"Come on Knitting. Let's march for the General."

She was enthusiastic about walking with me around the room. Even when the parade was over and the others were absorbed in painting and throwing wooden bricks and balls around the place, Knitting was beckoning to me to help her to walk some more.

When I stopped for a cup of jasmine tea, Mum told me about my new friend.

"Her real name is Shu Fang Zhou. The orphanage told me that she was born with weak, dislocated hips. Her mother and father had her adopted when she was about a year old because they couldn't cope with her. Then they were killed in a mud slide during a typhoon shortly afterwards. Maybe she was lucky to have been adopted and move away from her parents' shack. She would have been swept away with them. Sadly, her adoptive parents couldn't cope with her either, so she was returned to the orphanage.

"Anyway, the orphanage say that they have taken her to see specialists at the hospital who tell them that surgery would be pointless. Besides, it would be too expensive. The muscles around her hip joints are not strong enough. They have tried to relocate the joints, but they just pop out again. The situation is useless."

"But surely there is something that could be done. This is nineteen-seventy-three, Mum. Anything is possible these days!"

"Maybe if she belonged to some rich family you would be right. But there is no hope that she will ever walk unaided. You have to accept that."

To me, that was a challenge, especially after I had witnessed the little girl's determination. I was just as sure that she would walk as Mum was that she could never walk.

"From what you said, if her muscles were strong enough, her joints would hold in place and she'd be able to walk."

Kirsty just burst out laughing. "Who do you think you are, Calum? Doctor Kildare?"

"You're probably right, Calum, but it would take hours of physiotherapy to build that sort of strength in her hips."

Kirsty didn't believe me. Mum didn't believe me.

I shook my head and went back over to Knitting, who was sitting holding her arms out to me, begging me to walk her round the room once more.

Bless her! She's as certain as I am that she is going to walk. We'll do it together.

Chapter Seven

As we toured the nightclubs of Wanchai on Thursday evening, James and I encountered many of the US and Australian servicemen whom we had helped the previous evening. Without exception, they were happy to see us and very grateful for the service that we were providing. Some of them were so happy that they offered us cash for our cards which gave them "free" admittance to the Spitting Cobra. Mad fools! Still, it would have been rude to refuse their generosity and it was more money in our pockets.

All evening, I was thinking about our orphans and how we could improve the Day Centre. We needed more materials and could do with some equipment too. It was all very well relying on the generosity of the church congregation and our friends, but that would only ever be enough to keep us ticking over. Perhaps there was a way of getting these soldiers and sailors to contribute. They had plenty of money and they were all desperate to get rid of it. Even after they'd paid for their R&R recreational activities, they had plenty to spare.

I pledged to myself that I would speak to Mum about getting some flyers printed.

As usual, when we got back to the club, it was packed. Chen Wong was delighted.

"I'll see you tomorrow lunchtime for your payments. You have certainly earned your living. I already have high stacks of your cards sitting on my desk. How have you done this evening?"

James happily reported that we were both almost out of cards. "And we had more in our pockets when we set out tonight than we gave out last night."

"Excellent! You two are the best! I'll give you a few more boxes when I see you tomorrow."

When we'd got rid of our remaining stock of cards on introductions to the girls, we headed off down to Chater Road. I had mixed feelings when I couldn't see Hank in the crowd. I was disappointed because we couldn't continue our games with him, but I was pleased because we could chill out with all our friends and appreciate the great jazz that was being played by a local band, Spider Webb and the Cool Cats.

Kirsty was there with her new boyfriend, who she introduced as Ragnar Larsen. The guy was a huge Swede. He must have been half a head taller than me and I am six feet tall, or I like to say "five foot twelve" when I'm playing for a cheap laugh.

Ragnar was broad too. His long blond hair and thick ginger beard made him look much older than the rest of us. He was. I asked him his age with a direct question and he told me that he was twenty-one; three years older than me. It transpired that Iona had met him at a dinner party while Kirsty and I had been in England and had immediately thought that he would be ideal boyfriend material for my sister. She'd been telling him good things about Kirsty for a week and had finally managed to get them together. Kirsty seemed very happy about the arrangement.

I hit it off with him straight away. He was a lot of fun. His dad worked for one of the banks. I was interested to learn that his family had a boat moored round at Stanley and he had already invited Kirsty to go with him to an island for a barbecue sometime next week. They hadn't decided on a day yet.

"It would be great if you could come too, Calum. A few of your friends here are coming. Bring your girlfriend too, if you like."

I glanced at Iona, wishing that we were an item. "I don't have one just now, Ragnar. But I'd love to come along. Sounds like it'll be a lot of fun."

"Good. How about you James?"

"I don't know yet. It depends what day you go. I've got a few things planned for next week."

"That's OK. Just let me know."

He turned back to me. "I'll be picking Kirsty up from the front of your flats about eight o'clock on the day that we go. Obviously you can join us."

"Oh. You've got a car then?"

"No. I've got a Volkswagen camper van. It's a bit old and battered, but it gets me around."

I was excited. Although Dad had a very cool Sunbeam Alpine, which he just might let me drive sometime, this was even cooler than very cool. I was already thinking of the potential fun that we could have with Ragnar's van. We could take it up to Fan Ling, in the New Territories, and spend a few days up there.

"How many seats does it have, Ragnar?"

"Legally, I can take seven passengers, so eight altogether. I have actually managed to fit twelve in there in the past."

The seeds of an outrageous idea were beginning to sprout in the depths of my mind. We could do something very naughty to disrupt the forthcoming official opening of the Connaught Centre by the Governor, Sir Murray MacLehose. My thoughts were based on something that had happened when I had been a spectator at the charity rugby match between England and France at Twickenham earlier in the year. An Australian man had streaked straight across the pitch towards us and had been grabbed by couple of burly coppers, one of whom had used his policeman's helmet to cover the streaker's privates and restore some kind of modesty. Maybe some of my friends would be up to join me in a mass streak and Ragnar would drive the getaway van.

I decided to keep my idea to myself until I knew him a bit better and I had sussed out who might be willing to join me. The fewer people who were in on it, the better.

Some of my friends looked at me quizzically when I
burst out laughing at the thoughts that were whizzing
through my tiny mind. The number of people who could fit
into Ragnar's camper van was hardly the funniest joke in
the world. Little did they know!

Spider and his pair of Cool Cats had stepped down and
had been replaced by a pianist and a singer whom I had
never seen before. They were really good; soulful and
sultry. The mood of the room was changing. Although
there was still lots of drinking going on, the rowdiness had
dissipated somewhat.

* * * * *

The next morning, I could hardly wait to get down to
the Day Centre so that I could walk with Knitting. When
the children arrived, regardless of the activities that were
going on around us, I grabbed hold of her hands and
paraded her around the room. Although she couldn't speak
very well and the noises that she made were probably
closer to Cantonese than English, she found it easy to
communicate her happiness to me. In fact, whenever we
stopped for a break, she would demonstrate her frustration
and beg for more.

Mum was usually very positive but she told me that I
was wasting my time. Margaret and Kirsty were saying the
same. Knitting and I believed differently. She would walk.
Eventually, she definitely WOULD walk.

However, her legs were still crossing and uncrossing
and she was not bearing any weight at all as we
promenaded around. I tried to shake my own niggling
doubts as I defied my mother's opinions.

I took Knitting outside to the patio to avoid the
distractions and noise that everybody else was creating.
They were all having tremendous fun but so were we. And
we were on a mission. We would not fail!

Something remarkable happened while we were out there. As we went past a small wall that surrounded the base of a palm tree, Knitting pulled her left hand free from my grasp and reached towards the wall. I moved us closer and she grabbed hold of the top of the wall. She wanted to hold on with both hands. I knew her legs would collapse if she did so, so I was ready to catch her. Amazingly, she stayed on her feet which were very awkwardly poised. It only lasted a few seconds before she fell and I caught her.

We rushed inside and I told Mum.

"Rubbish, Calum. She couldn't possibly support herself on her legs. She must have locked her arms."

Regardless of what had actually happened, I was filled with hope.

When the minibus turned up to take the children back to the orphanage, all of them were, as usual, reluctant to go. But Knitting was even more agitated than normal. She cried. We had been on our feet for around four hours and she must have been tired. Nevertheless, she wanted to continue. When she'd gone, I cried too. Would she ever walk?

* * * * *

We met Dad for a late lunch at Les Quatre Temps Restaurant near the foot of the Peak Tram. I was quietly tucking in to my toasted club sandwich and Mum and Kirsty were busy telling Dad all about the antics of the children, when we were approached by a smartly turned out Chinese gentleman. Like Dad, he was immaculate in his pressed khaki shorts and white shirt, three-quarter length socks with garters and tabs and brushed suede shoes. It was the standard business dress in Hong Kong.

"Good afternoon Mister McDougal. I apologise for encroaching on your lunch with your family but may I join you? Hello Missus McDougal," he acknowledged my mother. Kirsty and I seemed to be invisible.

"Certainly, Mister Hom. Please pull up a chair. Would you like a drink?"

As he took his seat, Mister Hom accepted Dad's offer. "That's very kind of you. I'd like a green tea please."

Dad called the waitress over and ordered a pot of green tea for Mister Hom.

"So, what would you like to speak to me about?"

"I'll come straight to the point." He produced a fat, brown envelope and placed it on the table in front of my step-dad.

"I can see how fond you are of Missus McDougal and how proud you are of your two excellent children." At last he nodded towards us, acknowledging our existence. "Christmas is still months away. It's still the middle of summer," he laughed without conviction. "As I was thinking about your family it came into my mind that you might like to buy them a few presents in advance. You should be able to get all of them something very nice and something for yourself of course with the contents of the envelope. It is eight thousand, eight hundred and eighty-eight dollars." He flashed a huge smile of satisfaction to each of us in turn. We all understood the extreme quantity of luck that such a number carried in the Chinese culture.

Dad was silent. A thunderous frown creased his brow as he stared at Mister Hom. Although he was normally a very calm and tolerant man, I could see that Dad was very annoyed by this man's actions.

Mister Hom failed to register the waves of anger that were pounding towards him from across the table. He continued to smile like a manic clown.

Eventually, Dad spoke. His deep bass voice resonated, even though he spoke in quiet, measured tones.

"I am afraid that you have made a very big error Mister Hom. You should know better. If you speak with any of the other heads of engineering contractors in Hong Kong, they will freely tell you that the levels of bribery in the Colony upset me greatly. If you think that the contract for the retaining walls on the new Repulse Bay road can be bought, then...."

"Oh! It is not a bribe Mister McDougal! It is an example of my personal generosity because I would like to add some extra happiness to your family when it comes to Christmas."

"Do not interrupt me, Mister Hom. And do not take me for a fool. That was a blatant attempt at bribery. Please take your envelope and leave us."

Dad slid the brown envelope back across the table towards Mister Hom.

Mister Hom had turned quite pale.

"I assure you, M-mister McDoo..." he stammered.

He stopped speaking when Mum snatched the envelope and swiftly put it into her handbag.

Dad and Mister Hom glared at her, open-mouthed. Dad was confused and staggered by her action. Mister Hom was just staggered. He didn't know what to do or say. Kirsty and I were wondering what the heck Mum was up to.

She smiled. "Thank you very much, Mister Hom, for your extremely generous contribution to the Swallowfield Baptist Church Day Centre for Hong Kong Orphans. Eight thousand, eight hundred and eighty-eight dollars is going to buy us a lot of materials and equipment. This is just the boost we needed at this time. I cannot thank you enough."

Mister Hom continued to stare at her, open-mouthed. I chuckled as it crossed my mind that he was doing a fair impression of the large exotic fish in the tank behind his head. What could he say?

"Of course, we'll send you receipts for every cent that we spend and you will always be welcome to visit us at any time to witness the benefits that your wonderful donation will bring to those poor orphans. I am sure that they will appreciate it. They may even put on a little play or concert for you, to honour your contribution."

This made Mister Hom feel slightly better. He was probably already imagining the good publicity that his enforced gesture would surely bring. Perhaps there would even be a feature article in the South China Morning Post telling the public of his exceptional charitable donation and the difference that it had made to some of the poorest children on the island.

Dad soon knocked the wind out of his sails.

"As my wife said, we are very grateful for your donation. Unfortunately, the short list for the Repulse Bay Road contract has already been drawn up and your company's name does not feature. Good afternoon to you Mister Hom."

Totally deflated, Mister Hom rose, bade us all a polite "Goodbye," and left the restaurant.

As the door closed behind him, we all burst out laughing.

"That really was a master-stroke, darling," exuded Dad.

"Well done Mum!"

"Brilliant!"

We were all in a celebratory mood.

Suddenly, I remembered that I was meant to be meeting James down at the Spitting Cobra. It was already the middle of the afternoon. He and Chen Wong would be wondering where I was.

"Sorry Mum. I must rush now. I promised to meet James."

"You and James! I wish I knew what you got up to."

"I've told you, Mum," interjected my sister, not very helpfully. "They're gay!"

"We are not!"

"Now, now children!" Mum scolded. She turned back to me. "Just make sure you're home by about six, Calum. Wei Koo is cooking us your favourite tonight. She's got some fish from the market. Ikan goreng will be on the table at seven."

She was sure that such a high level of temptation would guarantee that I'd be home on time. There was no way that I could pass on a feast of ikan goreng. It really was my favourite dish in the whole wide world.

"I'll be there, Mum. I promise."

Kirsty was still grilling me hotly with her evil grin, knowing that she'd injured me with her "gay" comment.

Although it wasn't far, I jumped in a taxi to take me down to the night club. I was late. When I arrived, James and Chen Wong were chatting at the bar. Colin was busy polishing glasses and lining them up along the shelves. Three giggling girls were huddled around a table in a dark corner. As you'd expect, there were no customers at that time of day.

My friend was happy to see me and not at all annoyed by my tardiness.

"Sorry I'm late," I apologised to them both. I was witnessing yet another of my Mum's amazing ploys. I'll tell you about it later, James." I winked at my friend.

"No worries, Calum. James and I were just talking over a few ideas to bring in even more customers. Have a beer. Colin! A San Miguel for Mister McDougal please."

The stacks of our cards were neatly laid out on the bar in piles of fifty.

We were roughly even. James had two hundred and seventy eight to my two hundred and fifty eight. That meant that we'd get well over five thousand dollars each.

Chen Wong was extremely happy with us. "Your pile is worth $5,560, James. Calum, you earned $5,160. But I'm giving you six thousand dollars each. The business that you bring to the Spitting Cobra is worth much more than that."

We were delighted. I realised that it would take me more than four months to earn that amount once I started working for the Ben Line in January. I didn't care. I'd worry about that when I got to it. For now, it was all about having fun and sod what could happen in the future. James and I always tried our best to spend our money as fast as we could, within twenty four hours if possible. Usually, that was not possible.

We thanked Chen Wong and finished our beers. We left, saying that we'd be back "sometime next week."

On the way home, we popped into the Football Club for a quiet beer so I could tell James about Mum's encounter with Mister Hom. He thought that it was hilarious. So did I.

"Seriously though, that money is going to buy a lot of good stuff for the orphans, James." I'd told him about what went on down at the Day Centre. "I feel guilty though."

This was becoming a habit. I'd already been feeling bad about the poor people that I'd seen by the palace in Bangkok every time I ate a good meal. Now I was feeling bad about earning so much money for just handing out a few cards as we were celebrating my Mum's victory in gaining less than nine thousand dollars for the Day Centre.

I told James how I felt, and why.

"Forget it, Calum. Your Mum got them plenty of cash. Now we've got plenty of cash. We've earned that money. Let's just have a blast spending it like we always do."

"No James. I feel responsible for those orphans. I'm going to give half of mine to the Day Centre."

He roared with laughter.

"Ha ha ha! Who are you kidding? Since when have YOU acted responsibly?"

"Fair point. But I feel differently now. I want to do something for those kids. It is my duty to help them."

"It is your duty to help me to blow our fortune. We've got twelve thousand dollars between us!"

"Make that nine thousand. I am going home now and I am going to give Mum three thousand for the fund and tell her that we collected it from friendly American and Australian servicemen."

"Well, you wouldn't be lying, although none of them knew that they were donating to charity," he chuckled. "I am surprising myself, but I actually agree with you. In fact, give her four thousand. I am sure we can have a great deal of fun with the remaining eight thousand."

I hugged my friend. I was so happy.

* * * * *

As we sat down to dinner, Mum told me that she had some catalogues of equipment and toys and school materials such as paint, chalk, blackboards and so on. We could look at them after supper.

I spoke to her again about my hopes for Knitting.

"They make leg-braces for children, and adults, who have this kind of problem. The have a hinged bar attached to the ankles, so that their legs are kept separated."

"Shit! That sounds like medieval manacles to me. It sounds like a cruel torture."

"There's no point in buying them for Knitting anyway, Calum. The orphanage told me that they'd already tried it with her. It was useless."

"There must be other ways. She wants to walk. I can tell."

"Darling, you have to accept that she will never walk. That is the expert view. The surgeons know better than you, dear."

"No! I don't accept that. She will walk, Mum!" I was getting annoyed. My enjoyment of Wei Koo's ikan goreng was being ruined. "Please Mum. Let's discuss this after dinner."

She agreed.

I gradually calmed down. The fish was delicious. A few beers were helping my mood too. By the time we were sitting in the living area looking at the catalogues, my enthusiasm was restored.

Mum and Kirsty were looking at toy catalogues. I was more interested in some of the pharmaceutical equipment and mobility aids. There were plenty of walking frames and trolleys. I thought of how Knitting had supported herself, if only for a few seconds, on her arms on the small wall. Perhaps I could find a frame for her on which she could lean with her upper body and propel along by moving her twisted legs. It would be even better if I could find one with some sort of saddle in the middle which would force her legs to separate rather than cross as she moved along.

I had the design that I wanted in my head and I sketched it on a piece of paper. I marked a few frames which came close but lacked the centre piece that I was seeking. Perhaps Dad had an engineering friend who could adapt it for us to make it perfect for Knitting's walking lessons. I asked him about it.

"I'm not sure. The man who looks after our car has a workshop. He might be able to do it. We can go down there and speak to him next week. Let's see what he can do."

Yet again, Mum interjected to tell me that I was wasting my time.

Why does nobody else believe that Knitting can walk? I felt so frustrated.

I got myself another beer from the fridge and joined Mum and Kirsty amongst their piles of catalogues. Dad had dived back into his book: *The Silmarillion.*

My mind was distracted by visions of Knitting motoring around the room on the frame that I'd just semi-invented. I was turning the pages, browsing the pictures, but seeing nothing. I could not focus. That was when I turned a page to reveal an image that almost made my head explode. Well, not literally, obviously, but I felt a huge buzz of energy that was like an electric shock.

I stared at the picture of a toy horse. It had wheels for hooves and was designed for children to sit on and push along with their feet. It was called a "ponycycle." It didn't have pedals, as a bicycle would have. It had handles on the neck. I could just imagine Knitting sitting astride the ponycycle, holding herself up on the neck handles with her feet just touching the floor. With no strength in her legs, she would have to rely on me to push her along but maybe, just maybe, it would give her the impetus that she needed. It was perfect!

It was also very expensive at HK$ 900, but that was nothing to me. Thanks to Chen Wong and the Spitting Cobra, I was a man of means. Temporarily, at least.

"Look at this Mum!" I exclaimed, excitedly. "It is absolutely perfect for Knitting. This is just what she needs."

She looked at the page that I was showing her. "Yes. I agree with you. Full marks for your persistence. Even if she never manages to walk, this will be good to wheel her around on. How much is it?"

I pointed to the price.

"Gosh! That's a bit much. Remember that we have a limited budget. That one item, for one child, would cost us more than a tenth of Mister Hom's donation."

"I know. But we have a bit more than you thought."

"Really? How?"

"James and I were inspired by your success with Mister Hom. You thought that we were out on a pub crawl the last two nights, but we went round the bars in Wanchai and Central collecting donations for the Day Centre. Those Vietnam servicemen who are on leave are really generous. We managed to collect an extra four thousand dollars. I'll buy Knitting's pony out of that and give the remainder to your fund."

She found this amusing but I could tell that she was proud of us and absolutely delighted. "You really are a chip off the old block, aren't you? That's brilliant. We'll definitely put this ponycycle onto our list."

She scribbled "Ponycycle - $900" on her notepad.

Chapter Eight

The next morning, at the Day Centre, while the rest of us entertained the children, Mum and Margaret huddled over the catalogues and added more items to the list. Then they spent an hour or so on the telephone placing orders. I was delighted to hear that Knitting's pony would be with us before the end of the week. A small workshop in Sha Tin were making it to order so that it would be the right size for a six-year-old and would be adjustable to "grow" with her.

Mum was in a buoyant mood. She suggested that we take a trip out to Deepwater Bay when we'd finished at the Day Centre. We could swim in the sea and sit on the beach until Dad turned up later. He was going to be playing nine holes with Robert Millward, who I guessed must be Len's Dad. We could all have supper together at the Golf Club when they'd finished and showered.

It sounded like a good idea to us. Maybe some of our friends would come along. Kirsty asked Mum if that would be OK and she said that it would, but only while we were spending time on the beach. "You can't expect Dad to be buying supper for half of Hong Kong!"

Kirsty said that we'd go down to the Football Club and call Mum back at the flat from there to let her know what we were doing and how many of our friends were going to be coming along.

All of the usual gang were there and most of them wanted to join us for the trip to Deepwater Bay. We decided that we could go on the bus but Ragnar had a better idea.

"I'll go and get my camper van. We could all fit into that."

We were excited as he marched off towards Blue Pool Road to collect his vehicle.

When he'd gone, Kirsty went to the bar and called Mum to tell her of our plans. She soon came back looking a bit flushed.

"Mum is annoyed that we are leaving her to take a taxi to the beach on her own. I told her that you'd go home so that you could go with her, Calum."

"Well thanks a lot Sis! You go off in your precious boyfriend's van, while I have to walk up through the cemetery and ride out there with Mum."

"You're so sweet, Calum. I knew you'd understand," she sneered sarcastically. I jumped up, grabbed her, and threw her, screaming, into the pool. She deserved a ducking. Iona was laughing at me too, so I used that as an excuse to chuck her in too. I think that she enjoyed our grapple as much as I did.

As the pair of them returned, giggling, to the table, Kirsty reminded me that her "precious boyfriend" had promised to drive us all over to Stanley for a trip on his Dad's boat later that week. That was some consolation at least.

I got dressed and made my way up the hill taking the short cut through the graveyard.

* * * * *

Two hours later we were all sitting on the beach and having had a lot of fun in the water. These were happy times.

The conversation turned to the forthcoming grand opening of the Connaught Centre. It would be a big event. The tallest building in Hong Kong could hardly go unnoticed and the Governor himself would be doing the business, accompanied by his lady wife.

I was reminded of my idea for a daring streaking escapade. I needed to enlist some accomplices. There was no way that I was going to do it on my own. I was a bit wary of mentioning it in front of Kirsty, because there was a small chance that she'd blab to Mum rather than join the fun or just keep quiet. I also still had my doubts about Len, although he seemed as much up for a naughty prank as the rest of us.

I broached the subject gently by asking if anybody had seen news of that streaker at Twickenham back in February. There was immediate enthusiastic discussion about it. Everyone thought that it was brilliant. They had seen photos in the newspapers and on the front cover of *Private Eye*. They thought it even funnier when I told them that I, and a few of my friends, were in the background of a lot of those photos.

"We couldn't help it. He came running straight at us."

"Just like in that streaking song!" said Karen.

"What song?" I asked.

"*The Streak* by Ray Stevens. Haven't you heard it? 'Booga-dee booga-dee. Here he comes. Straight out of the cheap seats. DON'T LOOK ETHEL!'", she uttered in such a great impression that we all got it straight away.

"Yes. That's it." I paused. Looking around, I could see that they all thought that it was funny. "I've actually thought about streaking myself."

"Calum!" Kirsty exclaimed in mock horror. I could see that the idea of her brother doing something like that secretly appealed to her.

"It's just a case of finding the right time and place. I couldn't possibly do it on my own though. If we could think of an event to streak at, who would join me?"

James caught on immediately. "You're seriously not thinking of Sir Murray's big day at the Connaught Centre, are you?"

"Yes James. I am. You got it in one! Anybody else up for it?"

James, Len and Karen agreed straight away.

"You'll never get away with it," challenged Iona. "You'll get caught."

"I've thought about that, Iona. Firstly, I think that the surprise element will catch them out if we are quick. Secondly, I was thinking that we could have Ragnar waiting round the corner with his camper van, back doors open; we'd all jump in and Ragnar would put his foot down before anyone can chase us."

"I still think it's a risk, but that's part of the thrill. You can count me in."

It certainly would be a thrill. The idea of running naked down the street and jumping into a van with the gorgeous Iona was raising my blood pressure.

To my immense surprise, my sister raised her hands and said she'd join us too.

We still depended on Ragnar's cooperation. We all turned to look at him.

He hesitated. He looked around the circle for what seemed an age. I could almost hear the cogs of his brain grinding away. Eventually, and almost reluctantly, he confirmed, "Alright guys. I'll be your getaway driver."

We all cheered and laughed. We started planning. The option that we came up with was to find ourselves a spot to stand on the harbour side of the great building, dressed only in shorts and t-shirts - no underwear. We made a rule that trainers were allowed. The idea was to run naked, as fast as we could, from one side of the building to the other. If somebody stepped on something sharp with bare feet, it would ruin the whole escapade.

Ragnar would drive along the main road on the south side of the building at exactly five past eleven and stop at the side of the road with his four-way flashers on. When he was in position, we'd shed our clothes and drop them on the ground. Then we'd sprint across the broad pavement in front of the ceremony trying to avoid capture by the police. We were banking on them all being at the front of the crowd, near to the VIPs who were participating in the ceremony. Hopefully, we'd all arrive at the van within a few seconds of each other and pile into the back. As soon as we were all in and had slammed the door closed, Ragnar would head back to Happy Valley and Sports Road. We should all be sat around the pool enjoying a celebratory beer by half past eleven. That is if all went according to plan.

We were all very nervous, but very excited.

At that point, Mum came down to the beach to find us. "What's all the delirium about?"

"Oh, we were just talking about our next trip in Ragnar's van, Mum," answered Kirsty, quick as a flash.

I couldn't believe that she'd said that. Then I caught on. I was a bit slow.

"Yes. He's going to take us out to one of the islands on his Dad's boat. She's moored in Repulse Bay. We're planning a barbecue."

I must have looked guilty, even though my explanation had some truth in it.

"I see," she said, her voice laden with doubt. "And what is this boat called?" She directed her question at Kirsty and me rather than at Ragnar.

"Hoof Hearted," I answered, taking care to enunciate the gap between the two words.

Mum laughed. "Who Farted? That's so funny. I love it! Was that your idea, Ragnar?"

Her suspicion had been successfully deflected.

"No. It was my Mum's idea. This is the symbol on the bow."

In the sand he drew a horse shoe with a heart at its centre. We all giggled like little children do when somebody breaks wind in public.

"Dad's on the golf course. He should be finished in about an hour. We've booked a table for half past seven."

She spotted somebody she knew across the beach and excused herself to go and chat with her friend.

Chapter Nine

The following Monday morning, I was very disappointed to learn that Knitting's horse had still not arrived. Mum had called the factory in Sha Tin on Friday and had been told that the horse was being made to order. The first attempt had been made using the wrong specification. It would be too small for Knitting to use. They'd promised that the correctly sized horse would be ready for delivery on Monday. Now they were saying that they were very sorry but the person who made the horses was ill over the weekend and had not turned up this morning. He should be back on Tuesday or Wednesday and this would be his first job.

I was so upset that I decided it was high time for James and I to go on one of our gambling adventures to Macau. I knew he'd be up for it. I'd go down to the Football Club as soon as we were finished at the Day Centre.

Knitting was as enthusiastic as ever about trying to walk. She held her arms out to me. As she sat there on her chair, she was trying to lift her legs. Her right foot was actually lifting two or three inches. It seemed ridiculous to be excited by something so small but I was ecstatic. I had flash images going through my head of Knitting running around the room with the other children. This was a big breakthrough.

My heart was thumping as I led her around the room and out onto the patio. Once again, I took he over to the palm tree and rested her hands on the small wall. She definitely supported her own body weight. I walked her around the patio a couple of times, then back to the wall. She did it again! We repeated this a few times and went back into the room for a drink of water. Knitting was happy. How could I tell? She just could not stop laughing. Me neither.

I tried to tell her about the horse that was coming, but she had no idea what I was talking about or demonstrating, even when I started trotting around the room in the worst impression of a horse you ever saw. I gave up. She would see what I meant later in the week, hopefully as soon as I returned from Macau.

Knitting's progress had put me in a much better mood by the time I found James by the pool. As I expected, he was definitely ready for our next adventure. We arranged to meet outside the Royal Ascot Hotel at five o'clock. He went home. I waited for Kirsty so that I could get her to tell Mum not to expect me home for a couple of nights.

"Just tell her that I'm staying at James's. She'll create, but say that I'll see her on Wednesday." I thought about that. "Or maybe Thursday," I added to be on the safe side.

When my taxi pulled up outside the Royal Ascot, James was there waiting for me. We went straight into our well-rehearsed routine. This was such amazing fun.

We entered the hotel and boldly walked up to reception, hand-in-hand. I put on my campest voice as I asked for a double room. The young receptionist didn't dare ask any questions.

"Yes sir. Sa-sa-smoking or non-smoking sir?"

"Smoking please."

"Yes sir. We have a suite on the top floor, if you'd like that."

"No thank you. Just a simple double room, for one night, away from the street if possible."

"Please write your name and address in the book. I've got Room 325 on the third floor." She turned to pluck our key from the rows of hooks behind the desk.

"That sounds good, darling," said James, smiling. The poor receptionist looked as if she was about to faint.

I filled the next free line in the book with a false name, Alan Lim, and an address in down town Kowloon. The girl didn't even look at it. She was too alarmed by our relationship to say much more.

We thanked her as we took the key and made our way upstairs to our room.

As soon as we'd closed the door, we opened the bag and donned our white overalls. We disconnected the colour TV and headed for the service lift carrying it between us. When we got to the ground floor, we made for the back door. We encountered a chef who asked us, in English, who we were. James replied in fluent Cantonese.

"We're taking it back to the shop for repair. Manager knows. It'll be fixed by Wednesday. We left a replacement in the room till we get back. Must hurry. Goodbye."

The chef nodded and headed back to his kitchen.

The taxi that I'd arrived in just fifteen minutes earlier was waiting with its engine running. We put the TV on the back seat and I slid in next to it. James jumped into the passenger seat and ordered the driver to take us to the hydrofoil terminal in Central.

Two hours later we were in the pawnbroker's shop next to the Orion Casino in Macau, negotiating a price for the TV. There were always two prices: a lower-priced "buy back" option and a higher-priced "keep it" option. We always took the lower price.

The only place that officially allowed gambling in Hong Kong was the Jockey Club in Happy Valley. Although this was very convenient, being just a two minute walk from the Football Club, betting on a few horse races lacked the appeal of an all-night session in a Macau casino. It didn't fit into our adventurous plans either. A lot of the excitement was derived from the risks involved in borrowing a TV from a hotel, taking it to another country, pawning it and gambling with the proceeds. We didn't really even need the cash from pawning the TV, because we easily had enough from our nightclub escapades, but we were just having fun.

We bought some chips and split them between us before making our way to our favourite roulette table. We didn't really care if we won or lost, but winning would give us the thrill of buying back the TV and smuggling it back into the Royal Ascot with a passing "All fixed now!" in Cantonese, to any curious enquirer. If we lost, we'd go to the pawnbroker and scoop the difference between the "buy back" price and the "keep it" price, so that we could pay our hydrofoil fare back to Hong Kong.

Tonight, we were very lucky. By midnight, we were both over five thousand dollars up. Silverio Garrido, the manager of the casino, came out of his back room to chat with us.

"Are my people treating you well?"

"Yes. Thank you Silverio. We're being looked after," I replied.

We certainly were being very well looked after, as always. We were very privileged. Senhor Garrido had instructed his staff to serve us with alcoholic drinks and food at the table. This was a rarity among his customers. Very few people were allowed to do this.

I remembered our first visit to The Orion Casino in early 1973, very well. It had been a horrible experience, after what we believed was a good start. We had had more than our share of luck that night and it genuinely was very good luck. In just three hours we had made over twenty thousand dollars each. A smartly dressed manager had approached us and invited us into the manager's back office. Everybody was very civil and polite but as soon as we walked through the office door two huge men stepped into our path and punched us hard in our stomachs. We fell to the floor and suffered a severe kicking. There was blood flying everywhere. I could feel the bruises and my lips and nose were swelling and bleeding.

I was reeling as I was hauled off the floor and planted in a seat. James was beside me in another seat. He looked in a bad way.

Senhor Garrido entered the room.

"Tell me what is your system, unless you want some more of the same treatment."

He was direct, I'll give him that.

I struggled to reply. My mouth wasn't working properly.

"We ha... We haven't got any system, sir. We've just been lucky."

One of his thugs punched me again. It made me yell.

"Honestly, we have just been playing for fun and we managed to win," said James.

We continued to protest our innocence and received a few more painful blows for our trouble.

He insisted that we must have been cheating in some way. He told us that they had been watching us signalling to each other and could lip-read us as we told each other which numbers or combinations to bet on next.

For our part, we continued to insist that it must be beginners' luck, and it truly was. But every time we said that, we would be hit again. There seemed to be no way out of it.

Just when it seemed that we would suffer forever, Silverio waved his thugs aside.

"Boys. I believe you. I am very sorry for your beating but you must understand that I am often attacked by cheats. I have to protect my business. Please understand."

We were so relieved that we accepted his apologies. We never learned what had changed his mind.

"If you want to carry on playing, you are welcome to return to the tables. But I imagine that you will want to call it a night."

"Yes. You're right, Senhor," I replied. "I am very tired. And sore."

"Me too," said James, quite weakly.

"I am going to compensate you. We will give you double the value of your chips when you cash in. And we will put you up in our guest rooms tonight with whatever you desire to eat and drink. They are as good as you'll find in any five star hotel. I am really very sorry for what I've put you through. I want to prove that if you'll let me and I hope that you will return to The Orion. You will always be welcome here."

We were dazed as we discussed the events of the evening until the early hours of the morning. In the end, we decided that we would give the Portuguese man the benefit of the doubt and return in the future. Although he was very tough, he seemed genuine, and we felt that we would be treated well if we ever came back.

And so it had proved. Since then, we'd been treated like VIPs. But I'll never forget that horrendous beating. Nor will I forget the white lies that we had to tell to our parents to explain our bruised and swollen faces.

On this particular night, we agreed to play for another hour or so after Silverio had been out to check on our welfare. Happily, we won more and ended the evening, at about two in the morning, significantly in pocket. James had almost nine thousand dollars and I had a little more than seven thousand. We were already thinking of the fun that we'd have back in Hong Kong. We always challenged ourselves to spend all of our winnings within twenty four hours. That may sound easy, but it is much more difficult than you would think.

* * * * *

When we got back to Hong Kong, we headed straight for the Royal Ascot in a taxi with the colour TV on the back seat. We donned our white overalls along the way. Pulling up at the back door and tipping the driver handsomely, we made our way to the service lift and on up to our room. With the television back in its rightful place, we made our way down to reception and checked out.

Then it was down to the Star Ferry and across to Kowloon. We took a taxi to the Peninsular Hotel. The immaculately dressed doorman opened the taxi door for us as his colleague opened the boot to look for our luggage. We had none.

Before mounting the steps to the main entrance, we gave them a two hundred dollar tip each. They tried to keep straight faces as they gave us a polite, "Thank you, sir," but they found it difficult to hide their surprise and delight.

We walked straight to the reception desk and asked for the Presidential Suite.

"The Presidential Suite is occupied, sir. And so is the Peninsular Suite. The Marco Polo Suite is free, but it is very expensive."

"Perhaps you should not judge your patrons by their appearance. I am sure that we can afford it." I flashed a thick wad of hundred dollar notes. His eyes widened.

"Yes sir. I am very sorry sir. The Marco Polo Suite is ready for you. How many nights?"

"It is not a problem. Two nights please."

"Yes sir. Would you be kind enough to complete this form? Just your name and address there, your signature there and there."

I completed the form and told him that we would pay in advance, in cash. As he predicted, it was expensive. More so, as I pressed an extra five hundred dollars into his hand, thanking him for his kind service.

"The porter will take your bags to the room sir."

"We have no bags. We'll need to go shopping for some clothes. Please could you book us a car and driver to be outside at one o'clock?"

"Certainly sir."

"Make it a decent size. Big enough for four of us. And we'll need two classy women to accompany us. You understand what I mean?"

"Of course sir."

"Ask the ladies to come to the Marco Polo Suite in half an hour please."

"I'll do my best sir."

"Good." I gave him another hundred dollars and asked for the porter to show us to our suite.

Three porters were lined up, eager to help us. They had been watching, not very discretely. The receptionist called the name of one of them, probably his friend. They both knew that a good tip was on its way for simply riding in the lift to the top floor and back. And they were right.

Twenty minutes later there was a knock on our door. We'd had time to shower and clean up slightly. There were plenty of pleasant smelling creams and lotions in the bathroom so, although we were back in the clothes we'd had on for the last two days, we didn't smell too bad.

Our girls were gorgeous. Both were petite and Chinese. Their silky dark hair was shiny and smelt lovely as they stepped forward to kiss us in greeting. They introduced themselves as Dorothy and Mavis, which couldn't possibly be their real names. Or could they? I couldn't help thinking of them both as Doris and that made me chuckle. I am easily amused.

Dorothy started unbuttoning the front of her blouse as she danced seductively to some imaginary music.

"No! No!" exclaimed James. "Don't get undressed. We don't want you for sex. You are billed as escorts and that is exactly what we want you for. We'd like you to accompany us on a shopping trip. Come on. The limo will be out front waiting for us."

On the way down in the lift we paid them a thousand dollars each in advance. Their going rate was sixty dollars and hour, so they almost had a fit when they saw all that money.

Visiting plenty of the big stores in Kowloon with the limo taking us from one to another, even when it was only a few yards, was great fun. Dorothy and Mavis helped us to choose some new clothes for ourselves before we started splashing out on gifts for them. We had said that there would be no sex but resisting the temptation to let them come into the changing rooms with us to make sure that our new clothes, including underwear, fitted properly, was a temptation that was impossible to resist. It just resulted in some rather pleasurable groping.

The shop assistants sometimes objected or appeared to be outraged but a hundred dollar note soon had them flashing smiles, telling us that we were welcome and showing us to the most discrete cubicles.

Once we were both kitted out in expensive jeans and shirts and very flashy, patent leather shoes, we took the girls by their hands and led them through the arcades, past shops that sold furs and gold and sparkling jewellery.

"Do you like that coat, Doris? Er . . . Dorothy?"

"Yes. It's gorgeous!"

"How much is it? Can you see?"

"Yes. It's one thousand six hundred dollars."

"Here you are," I said, peeling off sufficient notes to buy the thick, luxurious fur coat. "Go and get it. It's yours."

She squealed and ran into the shop, laughing.

Minutes later, she emerged wearing the coat.

The rest of the afternoon was spent, frittering away our cash in the same manner. We had such a lot of fun.

By the evening, we had returned to the Peninsular Hotel to experience their fine dining. Although Jimmy's Kitchen was always the best in my opinion, the Peninsular was fantastic, and the prices meant that we would have no trouble burning all of our hard-earned cash.

Dorothy and Mavis couldn't believe their luck. We sent them packing at about ten o'clock. Normally, they'd probably be off to earn some more money but, due to our generosity and stupidity they would be able to take the next few days off.

Having been up and awake for almost two days, James and I took ourselves off to bed. In the morning, we decided to check out a day early and head home. By the time we'd paid, we had hardly any cash left. We gave most of what we did have away in tips. James was very happy to agree to my suggestion to spend the remainder at the market, buying food for the beggars who frequented the streets behind the rich façades of the harbour front. He had liked my account of what had happened to me in Bangkok and he readily joined me in my happiness in seeing the expressions on those people's faces as we handed over bags of fruit and vegetables.

When I got home, my mother was very angry.

"Where the hell have you been, Calum?" she yelled at me.

"Oh. Just having fun with James. We went to Macau."

"You went to Macau! Why?"

"It's an exciting place, Mum."

She slapped me on the top of my head, hard. It hurt. "Ouch!"

She slapped me again.

"Ouch!" again. "What was that for?"

"You know what it's for. What have you been teaching Pedro to say?"

"Nothing. I haven't been teaching him anything. He learns from what he hears, like when he calls Wei Koo in YOUR voice, Mum."

"Exactly! So when the washing machine starts its vibrating across the washroom floor and Pedro shouts, 'Shut that fucking racket up!' in YOUR voice, I hold you fully responsible."

I burst out laughing. So did Kirsty. It was a mistake. She slapped me again and glared at Kirsty.

Eventually, she saw the funny side and joined our laughter.

"Wait till I tell your Dad."

"Yes Mum. You know that he'll think it's funny too."

"You're right."

She paused, looking me up and down. "I suppose you're too tired and hung-over to come down to the Day Centre?"

"No. I want to come. I've missed two days with Knitting. Has her horse arrived yet?"

"Yes. It's there waiting for us. We haven't tried her with it yet. It was your idea, so we've left it for you to try. I don't hold out much hope but there is no harm in trying and it keeps you both occupied."

"She WILL walk, Mum. I know it! Knitting WILL
        walk!"

"We'll see," she said, disbelievingly.

Chapter Ten

I was so tired by the time we arrived at the Day Centre that I could hardly keep my eyes open. Mum and Kirsty were making concerned sidelong glances at me. I could tell that they were worried, even if they didn't want to show any outward signs of sympathy. To be truthful, I really didn't deserve any. I'd had a choice, and I had foolishly chosen to maximise my fun at the expense of sleep, wisdom and extravagance with the money that could have been much more wisely spent.

The sight of the toy horse soon woke me up. It was perfect for what I had in mind. I was so excited. Adrenalin went coursing through my veins in a sudden rush. I couldn't wait for the minibus to pull up outside to unload the children. When it did, I went straight over to help Knitting, carrying her into the hall. I knew that I was being slightly cruel to all the other children who were clamouring around me. I was ignoring them all but I only had one thing on my mind: to get Knitting onto that horse and have her shuffling around the room.

I could sense that she could feel my excitement and that she was curious about what was causing it.

I heard my mother's voice behind me. "Let them all settle down and have a drink first, Calum." I suffered a sudden bout of selective deafness. I just wanted to show Knitting her new apparatus without delay.

A puzzled expression appeared on Knitting's face as she looked at the ponycycle. She looked up at me and made some incoherent, enquiring noises. I knew exactly what she meant. We had developed an understanding; a language of our own.

The only way I'd be able to explain to her would be to actually show her. I sat her on the floor and indicated that she should watch me by pointing at her, then at my eyes, then at my chest. I stood astride the horse, which was far too small for me, and placed my hands firmly on the front rail. I slowly moved my right foot forward a few inches followed by my left. I rolled the horse forward a corresponding amount. By the time I'd repeated the operation a couple of times, Knitting was bouncing up and down on the floor and laughing. She wanted to have a go.

I was happy to oblige by helping her to mount her new steed. I had to push her along as she had very little power in her legs, but she was trying very hard to make contact with the floor and gain some traction. I was delighted and filled with hope. I'm no fool though. I knew that it was going to be a long slog.

It was obvious that Knitting was also delighted. For the first time in her life she was propelling herself forward without the handicap of her legs crossing. I could see that she was determined to continue and she believed that she would eventually walk. So did I. We just needed to persevere and build her strength where she previously had none.

When we stopped for a break and a drink of water she was eager to get back in the saddle. Before she did so I had an idea. I lifted her feet in front of her as she sat in her chair and indicated that she should push against my hands. I put her through a cycling motion. I could feel some resistance. I am no professional physiotherapist but I thought that this might be the sort of thing one would do if we could afford such services.

After a while we returned to the horse. This was to be our pattern for many weeks to come and she never lost her enthusiasm. Mum was slightly miffed that I was giving most of my attention to one child but she had become my project. I was passionate about the goal of seeing Knitting walk.

I didn't neglect the rest of the children entirely. I couldn't. Besides, I enjoyed marching up and down for

General Cheung too much. And our little impromptu plays and musicals were hysterical. Everybody took great pleasure in splashing paint around and making a lot of mess with clay.

The greatest fulfilment for all of us came from soaking up the happiness of these handicapped orphans as they participated in the entertainment. Far from being tiring, keeping the activities going seemed to energise us.

Chapter Eleven

We got into a routine. As soon as we'd finished at the Day Centre, we'd walk down to the Football Club to lounge around with our friends by the pool for the afternoon. I'd occasionally accept a challenge to a game of squash from one of my friends or another member of the club. I was decidedly average at the game and lost more games than I won. That didn't usually bother me too much, as I only played for fun, but being beaten by one of the older committee members, Clive Morris, who was rather portly, really rankled. He was so unfit, yet he could stand in the middle of the court, barely taking more than one step in any direction, and force me to run around the walls like an angry wasp in a jar. Curse him!

To give Clive his due, he would never accept the beer that I always offered to him for his victory. Quite the contrary. He would come straight over to the pool bar and put drinks for our whole group onto his own tab. I resented him for beating me but liked him for looking after us.

Quite often our lazy afternoon sessions would evolve into a night out down town.

I remember one particular Wednesday very well. James and I thought we'd head for the Godown for a quiet early beer and then we would decide where to go on to from there. We were very surprised at how quiet it was. Even at six o'clock on a midweek evening there were usually a few people sitting around chatting.

In the shadows of one of the booths sat a very lonely looking figure. When we'd got our drinks, we walked past him towards our favourite table. As we did so we recognised the man. We were shocked!

It was none other than Hank, the American sailor whom we had encountered three of four week ago.

"Hi Hank!" James greeted him. "What are you still doing in Hong Kong? I thought you only had two weeks of R&R."

"Hi guys. You're right. I did. But I fell sick with appendicitis and spent a few days in hospital. My ship sailed without me. I'm on shore duty for six weeks before I can join a new ship."

"I don't know whether to commiserate with you or congratulate you on good timing with your illness," I said.

"Oh! I'm fairly happy to be spending a few more weeks here and the ship's company of my old ship were a bunch of jerks anyway. They used to pick on me at every opportunity."

I wondered why. Perhaps Hank was actually the only jerk in the crew.

"But there's another unexpected upside," exclaimed Hank.

"Oh yes. What would that be?" asked James.

"Don't you remember our drinking challenge? I'll bet you guys thought you'd got away with that one. Well here I am and I'll be more than happy to take free drinks off you all night." He paused, scrutinising our faces. "Unless you're going to chicken out like typical Limeys." He laughed loudly.

We looked at each other and shrugged simultaneously as if to say, "Why not?" To be honest, we had also thought that we'd lost our opportunity to drink this loud-mouthed idiot under the table and put him in his rightful place.

"I think you'll be the one who ends up paying, Hank, but we're definitely up for it. What's your tipple?"

"Bourbon!"

"Fair enough. I'll drink whisky and James likes rum."

"Let's just go over the rules again before we start. We told you last time we saw you but it's good to be sure that we all know what we're playing for."

James and I had thought this through. We'd also briefed Steve, the barman, who was an old friend.

"OK. Shoot!"

"We each put our wallets, sorry, pocket books, in the care of the barman. We drink our chosen spirit, one-for-one, until one of us admits defeat, or collapses from the effects. The barman will take the total bill out of the loser's wallet. That'll be you, Hank."

He laughed again. "I very much think not!"

"Just in case it is, you'd better write down your address, so we can get you home in a taxi. Where are you staying?"

"Don't think I need to write it down for you. You must know the British Naval base, HMS Tamar?"

"Of course. Don't tell us that those lousy Limeys allow US Navy personnel on their base. I hope that they look after you."

"Yeah. Not bad, I s'pose."

"Anyway, we'll make sure you get back to the base safely."

"It won't be me who'll need a taxi. Let's get this game going." He threw his wallet on the table. James picked it up and took it with mine and his own up to the bar. He soon returned with a Bourbon, a Scotch and a rum.

We grabbed our drinks, tapped them on the table and, with a chorus of "Yum sing!" downed them in one. As soon as the empty glasses were back on the table Hank grabbed them and headed for the bar for the next round.

The strength of my drink had put doubts into my mind about whether Steve had remembered the instructions that we'd given him more than three weeks before. I discretely asked him as I collected the third round.

He whispered back to me, "Don't worry, Calum. I just couldn't do it with the Yank watching. All your drinks, and James's, will be half strength when you and James come to the bar. Matey Boy's will all be full on."

After we'd had about three rounds each, James and I were tapping the table, calling the customary "Yum sing!" and, as Hank tossed his drink down his neck, we were tossing them over our shoulders. The poor guy didn't stand a chance. It wasn't long before his eyes started to roll, yet he was still taunting us with cries of, "Bring me another one! You Brits are going to fall like you did at the Boston Tea Party!"

Thirty minutes later, Hank slumped forward onto the table unconscious. James lifted him by a handful of the little hair he had, then dropped his head back onto the table. It bounced. We had him.

"We'd better take him down to Tamar, Calum."

"Maybe we could take a little diversion along the way, James," I suggested.

"What do you mean?"

"I've been thinking that Hank is such a complete prick that we have to penalise him a bit more than just taking the money for the drinks from his wallet."

"Have you got something in mind?"

"Yes. Why don't we take him down to see our friend, Annie, at Tao An Ink? We could pay for a lovely British tribute tattoo for him out of his own money."

James laughed loudly. "Yeah! That's a great idea Cal." He paused. "But don't you think it's a bit mean? He'll have that tattoo on his skin for the rest of his life."

"But he deserves it, James. He's such an arrogant twat. He might actually learn a little humility out of this and he'll certainly never forget this evening."

"You're right. Let's do it. But, knowing what we know of Hank, I have a feeling that he'll make up a good story so that he can dine out on this for the rest of his life."

"Maybe."

We paid Steve and tipped him handsomely out of Hank's wallet, which was bulging with hundred dollar notes. Then we climbed the stairs up to the street to hail a cab. Five minutes later we were being greeted by Annie. Fortunately, she was not busy.

We chatted about some ideas with her, aiming for the ultimate. Eventually we stripped off his shirt and laid him face down on Annie's padded table.

"It's going to take me about three hours. Do you want to come back later?"

"No. We'll stay here and drink coffee. We want to stay sober so we can take him back to his base safely. And we can enjoy the view while we're waiting."

We paid her double her requested fee in advance and put the kettle on.

She was a true artist. In a little over an hour she had all of the line-work done and was ready for the colouring and shading. It looked wonderful already.

Filling the canvas of his whole back she'd inked a laurel wreath. Across the centre was a wide banner, inscribed "BRITANNIA" in an Old English font. Above the banner, in beautiful, flowing script, the words "I love". And below the banner, in matching script, "Limeys".

We couldn't stop chuckling and imagining Hank's shock in the morning and how he might explain this away to his friends, if he actually had any.

We felt wicked and I suppose we really were.

Once the laurel leaves were shaded with green ink and the rest of the tattoo had been nicely coloured too, the result was very impressive. Annie padded her work of art with plenty of pink tissue and we replaced Hank's shirt. He was still unconscious but he was starting to moan a little. We had to get him down to the gates of HMS Tamar as quickly as possible.

The sentries took charge of him when they saw his ID card. They were obviously used to receiving drunken sailors who had over-indulged. They promised to take care of him and thanked us for being so thoughtful in bringing him back.

"You might have saved his life. You never know what could've happened to him if you'd left him just lying in the street."

We couldn't wait to tell our friends about this when we met them at the club the next day. Our report of what had been a very satisfactory evening would provide much hilarity.

* * * * *

We were right. Almost all of our friends thought it was absolutely hilarious. I have to say "almost," because Len proceeded to put a damper on it.

"Don't you think that the police could come after you and charge you with GBH or ABH?"

"No. He had it coming. It was self-defence," joked James.

"You may laugh, but..."

"Thank you. Ha ha ha ha!"

"You should take this a little more seriously. I really believe that you have committed a crime. It may seem like a joke to you two but you have paid for somebody to be injured for life, whether he likes it or not."

"Come on Len. We did that guy a favour. He likes to have the best of everything and he now has one of the finest tattoos that anybody could wish for. We should have added to it's value by getting Annie to sign it. She's world famous in Hong Kong."

"You're still not taking this seriously enough, Calum. I am only trying to help. It's best to be prepared just in case you do feel the long arm of the law."

"Shut up, Len," said Iona, sticking up for us. "It was only a bit of fun."

As usual, I was distracted by her gorgeous, bikini-clad body as soon as she spoke and almost missed Len's next comment.

"I'll ask my Dad when I get home this evening. He knows lots of police officers and lawyers. He's bound to know if you can expect any trouble."

James and I looked at each other, askance at Len's outrageous suggestion.

"Are you mad?" I exclaimed. "That's asking for trouble."

"Why would you open a possible can of worms for us when there is no need at all for it?" asked James.

"Ah! So you admit that you might have done something wrong then?"

"No. But you don't need to say anything to your Dad about it, do you?"

"Alright. As I said, I was only trying to help."

"Well, thanks Len, but please don't." I changed the subject. "Are we still planning a trip on your Dad's boat Ragnar?"

Ragnar looked across at Kirsty before replying. They smiled at each other. It felt like a conspiracy.

"As a matter of fact, I was going to ask you all to come this Saturday, if you can make it."

There was immediate excitement. We all wanted to go along. The rest of the afternoon was spent discussing our plans for the trip. Everyone wanted to contribute some food or drink for the barbecue. Ragnar made a list of where he would pick each of us up and what we'd be bringing to the party. It would be an early start so that we could get away from Stanley to one of the remote islands or coves and make the most of the day.

As I walked home through the cemetery with Kirsty, I was worrying about what Len had said. Would he speak to his Dad about what James and I had done to Hank? Could we really be in trouble with the law?

Chapter Twelve

I was feeling much more positive by the time Kirsty and I were standing outside our block of flats on Stubbs Road waiting for Raglan's camper van to come around the corner on Saturday morning. We'd had to get up at six and we were bleary-eyed and far too tired for conversation. I was reflecting on Knitting's incredible progress. Already, she was able to gain more traction and put more weight on her feet as she propelled herself along on her horse. I could hardly believe it.

Helmut, Iona, James and Karen were already on board. I was surprised to see Janet, another friend of Kirsty's who I'd thought was still in England. Kirsty and Janet immediately started screaming and hugging. I felt sick. For a second I thought about screaming sarcastically and hugging James like a girl who hadn't seen her friend for three weeks, but then I thought better of it. It would have been a futile joke and it would have put me in my sister's bad books for the rest of the day.

As Raglan drove us over Wong Nai Chung Gap and past Deepwater Bay, we chatted about the food and drink that we'd brought, hoping that we wouldn't have to stop to buy anything before we boarded *Hoof Hearted*. It turned out that we probably had far too much.

Karen, as usual, had found the seat next to me. I knew that she fancied me but, although I liked her very much, I had my eyes on Iona. However, I had to admit that I was rather enjoying the way that she deliberately leaned in to me as we went round every bend on the twisty road. I almost jumped out of my skin as we ascended the hill just past Repulse Bay. She leaned right across me and screamed at the top of her voice, nearly causing Raglan to almost drive off the road.

"Stop! Raglan! Stop!"

"He pulled over to the side of the road."

"What's wrong? Are you going to be sick?"

"No. Look! Look down there."

She pointed down at the sea.

Now I understood. What we saw was truly awesome. Six giant rays were swimming in formation across the bay only fifty yards out from the shore. It looked as if they were flying, very gracefully, through the sea.

We were all amazed by the sight. It was something that I would never forget.

Eventually, they disappeared from view and Raglan continued the drive down into Stanley.

Hoof Hearted was an amazing little cruiser. Real luxury. There was plenty of room on board and she had a decent galley with a cooker and a large fridge. There was a lounge with padded seats and tables. In the open deck there were more padded seats toward the stern and lots of room for us all to stretch out and sunbathe on the fore deck. There was even a shower on the fore deck too. *Hoof Hearted* had a roomy fly deck with modern, easy-to-use controls. She was a far cry from the ancient pinnace on which I had learned my seamanship skills in the Menai Strait.

We were soon lounging around in our trunks and swimsuits and glugging on cold bottles of San Miguel as Raglan steered his boat out to sea.

After about half an hour, we anchored about a hundred yards off the golden beach of a small island which appeared to be uninhabited. Before the *Hoof Hearted* had even swung round and come to rest, we were diving off into the warm, clear water. There were plenty of masks and snorkels on board, so three or four of my friends were swimming around admiring the colourful fish.

I challenged James to dive to the bottom and fetch a rock or shell to prove that he'd made it. He tried and failed. I tried and failed. He climbed up to the fly deck and dived into the water. When he surfaced he was triumphantly holding a sea urchin above his head.

"Beat that Calum!"

I couldn't let that rest. I climbed up onto the fly deck and dived off. I could see the bottom and swam towards a hand-sized clam. Suddenly, my face, arms and shoulders started stinging painfully. It was a huge shock. I pulled myself quickly to the surface, almost panicking. I climbed aboard at the stern, yelling at my friends.

"What the fuck is this!"

"You've got tentacles all over you Calum," Iona told me. "Quick. Come to the shower."

She grabbed the on-deck shower head and stamped on the large rubber button on the deck.

Between us, we rubbed the tentacles off me, but the stings were worse than any pain I'd ever felt. They were definitely worse than nettle or wasp stings. And they were leaving white weal marks all over my body.

Some tentacles were caught in the silver chain around my neck. It was the one that my mother had bought me in Perth when I was about thirteen. Suspended from is was a small silver Celtic cross with embedded green stone. Iona removed it.

I was still in great pain and trying to wipe off tentacles which were no longer there.

"I think we've got them all off you. I'll ask Raglan if he's got any cream that we can use. Sit down and drink some water. No alcohol!"

She was being very serious and stern. I had little choice but to obey.

A couple of minutes later she returned with a tube of cream.

"This is for insect bites and stings but I'm sure that it will soothe the jellyfish stings for you."

"I hope so. This is agony, Iona."

I went to take the tube from her but she snatched it away from me.

"Here. Let me."

I allowed her to rub the cream into my stings, which were everywhere. The pain started to turn to pleasure as the girl that I had fancied for some time rubbed cream all over my body. She seemed to be enjoying the experience too.

"We must do this more often, Calum!" she joked.

I had to confess that I had dreamed about it. Spontaneously, I told her that the last time she had come for a sleep-over and stayed in Kirsty's room, I had been hoping and praying that she might wander into my room during the night.

"I had the same thought but was too nervous.I was really tempted, Calum. Maybe next time."

My pain was rapidly disappearing as my mind raced ahead, contemplating the prospect.

"I'll get you some more water. Stay there."

My other friends were showing concern for me too. Although the pain was subsiding, the weals across my body were not and they looked quite angry. I wallowed in their pity, enjoying the moment.

Iona returned with the water. She produced my chain and fastened it around my neck.

"Is that Iona stone?" she asked, pointing at my cross.

"Yes it is!" I had never made the connection before. She had never noticed it before.

"I've seen your cross but I've never looked so closely at the stone. It's lovely."

"Thanks Iona. Mum got it for me years ago when we visited the Island of Iona, off Mull. It is very special to me. It's even more special now."

She smiled. I melted.

* * * * *

The sympathy of my friends didn't last very long. After we'd rustled up something to eat we agreed that we should all swim ashore and go for a walk around the island.

James was wise enough to advise that we should wear shoes and watch out for snakes.

"They'll slither away when they hear us coming but if one of them is dozing in our path it would be easy to step on and get bitten."

"I've got some antivenom and syringes in the first aid kit but I'd rather not use it," volunteered Raglan.

"We should take it with us, just in case," said Karen.

"Let's just be careful," I said. "I've already had enough today with the jellyfish stings. I don't want any of us to add a snake bite to our casualty list."

Some of them laughed. Iona grabbed my hand and squeezed it. That was exactly the result that I'd been seeking.

As we walked up the path from the beach we didn't see any snakes but we saw lots of colourful birds. Karen spotted a praying mantis and Len pointed out a bright green lizard that was doing its best to flatten itself to a tree trunk so that we wouldn't notice it. Its problem was that it was bright green and the bark of the tree was brown. It scuttled off as soon as we got too close.

We reached the top of a ridge and were shocked to hear and see a mass fight occurring in the valley before us. We ducked down and watched, horrified. The fighting was really vicious, and bodies were lying all over the clearing. Within three or four minutes there was just one man left standing. He was barefoot and naked from the waist up.

We were all looking at each other, wondering what to do, when applause broke out from the woods below us and people emerged wearing normal shirts and shorts. The prostrate bodies suddenly revived, jumping to their feet and chatting to each other and laughing.

It became obvious that we were observing a film set.

We rose to our feet and made our way down to the clearing.

The crew were surprised to see us. A smart-looking man came over to us. He had realised that we were probably shocked by what we had witnessed.

"Sorry guys. We were pretty sure that there was nobody else on the island. Where did you spring from?"

"My friend's boat is moored in the bay on the other side of the island," I replied, pointing at Raglan. We're just here on a day out. What are you filming?"

"It's the latest Golden Dragon film starring Bruce Lee. It'll be screening early next year. I can't say much more than that. My name's Robert. I'm directing this movie. Would you like to meet Bruce?"

I could see that everybody else was as excited as I was. My sister even squealed.

"Yes please Mister . . . erm . . . Robert!"

The director took us over to Bruce who asked each of us our names and a few questions such as "Do you live in Hong Kong or are you here on holiday?" We were all awe-struck at meeting this great star. Initially, we struggled to answer him. He was such a humble man and he spoke to us as if we were his equals. We soon relaxed in his company. He invited us to sit in the shade under the trees for a longer chat.

"I've got plenty of time before my next scene."

It was an amazing conversation and one that I'll remember forever. He told us that he liked to go out in Kowloon with his friends for a quiet night and that he didn't like being noticed but it was really difficult to escape recognition. He was often harassed by people who did not believe in his martial arts abilities. He said that it had taken a lot of hard work and dedication to perfect his talent and he was very disciplined in its use. He would never even consider getting into a real fight.

He volunteered to show us a little "party piece." He got his aides to set up two vertical bamboo poles with a cross-bar of bamboo, about one inch in diameter, secured above my head height. Bruce himself was about four or five inches shorter than me and I am six feet tall. He crouched beneath the stick and told us to watch carefully. After what seemed like an age, he sprang high into the air, his limbs whirring in a blur. The stick snapped. To me, he hadn't appeared to have even touched it.

Drawing himself up to his full height, he asked us with which part of his body we thought he'd broken the stick. We each hazarded a guess.

"Your hand."

"Your head."

"Your elbow."

"Your knee."

When we'd finished guessing, he raised his right foot to show us a white mark on the outer sole. I was amazed and so were my friends.

He stayed chatting with us for a few more minutes before Robert called him over for the next shoot. We thanked him for speaking to us and said goodbye. As we made our way back to the beach and the boat, we talked enthusiastically to each other about our encounter with the great man. We all agreed that Bruce Lee was a very likeable man. Little did we know that a few weeks later, he would be dead. It was an unforeseen tragedy.

Chapter Thirteen

Mum squealed with excitement as she looked past me into the room full of children. It was most unlike her to show such a lack of control.

"Look Calum! Look at Knitting!"

My heart leapt into my mouth. I had only just left her alone for a few seconds to walk to the table and take a sip from my Cream Soda bottle. I turned, expecting to see Knitting lying on the floor with her horse on top of her. But what I saw amazed me too. In a flash, I understood Mum's excitement.

Knitting was pushing the horse across the floor, leaning on the front bar and using her feet and legs to move the equipment. This was a huge breakthrough.

"Look at her. You've only been working with her for less than three months, Calum. It's paid off."

"I always knew it would, Mum," I answered. "I was always sure this day would come. And I am sure that she will walk soon too."

"For the first time, I believe that you could actually be right. I admit that I had doubted you all along. This is remarkable. You've done something wonderful when nobody, NOBODY, believed that you could do it. Well done Calum!"

Knitting had stopped and was looking round at me, a huge grin spreading across her face.

I was speechless. I was trembling. My chest swelled with pride. Not for me, but for her. I turned back to Mum, a grin to match Knitting's on my own face.

It was a few seconds before I could speak.

"That's where you're wrong again, Mum. I wasn't the only one who believed it. The main person who believed it, and the main person who made this happen, was Knitting herself."

Realisation lit Mum's face like a beacon on a dark night. She knew that what I was telling her was the truth. She didn't need to tell me what she was thinking. I knew. It was enough for me.

I turned and took the three short steps across to my heroine. I picked her up and hugged her. She just laughed. We were both so very happy.

Knitting couldn't talk, at least not in words that I understood, but she could certainly laugh. She always laughed when she was happy or when she'd achieved something. She knew that what she had done was very special. I had never heard her laugh so much.

All of the helpers, and most of the children, joined in with her celebrations.

I spent a further half an hour walking around with her, holding her hands. She had got into a habit of separating her legs as she walked, and was bearing much more weight. I knew that if I let go of her hands she would fall, but she was making such wonderful progress. I took her out to rest on the wall around the palm tree. I remembered that day when she had first supported herself there. It seemed so long ago.

We went inside and saw that everyone was participating in what had become a regular ritual at the Day Centre: General Cheung's march past. I put Knitting back on her horse and pushed her past the saluting Fai Cheung who was proudly wearing my naval officer's cap.

I was surprised when Cheung jumped down off his rostrum and came over to me and Knitting. He removed my cap and placed it on Knitting's head. He stepped back and saluted her.

"Shu Fang Zhou!" he shouted. He used her real name. "Salute!"

All the other children saluted her as best they could and shouted out her name or approximations of it. I was touched by their behaviour.

* * * * *

Kirsty and I couldn't wait to get to the Football Club to tell our friends about Knitting's breakthrough. As we expected, they were excited when they heard the news.

"I'd love to come down to see her," said Karen.

"Me too," added Len. "It would be great to see all of these kids that you keep telling us about."

"You can all come down at any time," Kirsty told them."Mum always welcomes new volunteers." She grinned cheekily.

"I knew you'd do it, Calum," James said, punching me on the arm.

It was true. He was the only other person who had believed in me and Knitting.

"Thanks James. But she hasn't actually walked yet."

"She will though. Look at the progress she's made in just three or four months."

"You're right. We'll keep going until she walks on her own, even if it takes a year."

Clive Morris came over to our table to ask what we were all celebrating. We told him.

"That is truly amazing, Calum. Well done! Let me buy you all a drink."

"That's very kind, Mister Morris. We'll have another jug of Gunners please."

Gunners was my favourite refreshing drink: half ginger beer, half ginger ale, a teaspoonful of Angostura Bitters and a handful of sliced lime. Delicious!

* * * * *

We were still having a lot of fun around the pool when Mum and Dad arrived at about six o'clock. Mum announced that we'd have supper at Sammy's Indonesian restaurant, just around the corner in Leighton Road.

She slammed a copy of the South China Morning Post on the table.

"Perhaps you can explain this, Calum? Or any of you?"

"What?"

"This! Look!"

We looked down at the photo that went with the headline, "Streakers Disrupt Connaught Centre Opening". We couldn't help laughing.

"That's quite funny, Mum. I wonder who they were."

"Don't give me that. It's clear that it is you lot. Where were you yesterday afternoon?"

We tried to deny it for a few minutes, but our efforts were futile. Besides, it had been such fun. I was chuckling even more as I remembered the look of shock on the faces of the crowd and the police officers as we'd dashed past the Governor and his wife. They had been so stunned that nobody had given chase, and we'd made it into Ragnar's camper van and away before anyone moved to stop us. Then there was the tangle of naked limbs as we scrambled to find out clothes and get dressed as the van whizzed around the corners on the way back to Sports Road and safety. There'd been plenty of surreptitious groping going on in those few minutes that it took us to arrive at our destination.

"You should all be ashamed of yourselves! It's not funny!"

"They were just having a bit of fun, Sheena. I don't think that the police are taking it seriously, and most of Hong Kong are laughing about it, even Sir Murray MacLehose himself."

"That's not the point, Donald. Think of what our friends will be saying. You can see that that's Calum and Kirsty in those photos. And James is easily recognisable too."

"Our friends are probably having a good laugh about it too. Come on. We've all got up to high jinx in our time. Even you, Sheena."

"Humph!" Mum stormed off towards the bar. She was seriously annoyed.

"Don't worry. She'll see the funny side of it eventually," said Dad as he turned and followed her.

We all burst into uproarious laughter, which probably annoyed Mum even more.

"She should learn to lighten up," said my sister.

She was right, but I admit that I was feeling a bit nervous about Dad's mention of the police, even though they didn't appear to be concerned.

My thoughts strayed back to the promised supper in the restaurant where our amah's husband worked. I knew what I would be eating. I almost always went for the *ikan goreng*. It would never be as good as the version that Jannah, our amah in Borneo when I was seven, had cooked for us. I could remember her rolling the white fish in crushed red spices, wrapping it in an envelope of banana leaf, and throwing it into the embers of an outdoor fire. After about fifteen minutes she would take it out and split it open with her parang. Kirsty and I would tuck in using our fingers.

Ikan goreng was still my favourite dish in the whole world. The chef in Sammy's restaurant did a great version of the dish, and I loved it and never missed the opportunity to consume it.

The problem with Mum's proposal was that Kirsty had a date with Ragnar. To complicate matters, they had asked me and Iona if we'd like to make it a foursome. They wanted to try out the new English pub in Central, The Blue Moon. Yet another opportunity not to be missed.

So I had to choose between two unmissable opportunities.

I asked Iona and Raglan if they would be willing to wait for us to return from supper. They looked at each other before Raglan replied.

"It depends how long you are. Go to supper and come back here afterwards. If we're still here, we can go on to The Blue Moon for a few drinks. If not, we'll see you tomorrow."

Iona smiled and nodded her agreement.

We went to join Mum and Dad at the bar.

"How long do you think we'll be, Mum?" asked Kirsty.

"Why darling? Does it matter?"

Kirsty explained our dilemma and that, although we were eager to eat at Sammy's, we'd like to get back to spend the rest of the evening with our friends.

Dad immediately came up with a great solution.

"Raglan and Iona can come to dinner with us. Go and ask them. Tell them that I'll pay." He smiled. Kirsty skipped happily back to the pool and soon returned with her boyfriend and my girlfriend.

Dad could be so generous and understanding.

As usual, we were made to feel very welcome at the Dapur Kampung. It was almost as if we were family. Sammy and the other waiters were like brothers. They were always so cheerful and friendly. Once we were settled at the table with some drinks, the chef came out to chat with us about what we might like to eat. My main course never varied, but he always asked me.

The meal was perfect. Between the main course and the dessert, Mum had her customary cigarette. She always cracked the same cringe-worthy joke: "I never miss my intercourse!" When she'd extinguished her cigarette, she started on her usual dessert: sweet coconut slab, even though she always moaned that is was far too sweet. It never ceased me to amaze me that she could moan about something that she so obviously enjoyed.

* * * * *

Raglan and Iona thanked Dad profusely before we left Mum and Dad to enjoy their liqueurs and made our way outside to find a taxi to take us to The Blue Moon.

The place was packed when we got there, but we found a table in the corner for the four of us. It was just like a stereotypical English country pub. I went to fetch the first round of drinks and returned to the table with four pints of draught bass.

It was good to relax with friends.

"Your Mum didn't seem too impressed with our streaking yesterday," Raglan said to Kirsty and me.

"No. She was really annoyed," added Iona.

Kirsty laughed it off. "Ach. She isn't worried about the police, it's more what her posh friends will think of it."

"She'll come round when she realises that everybody else thinks that it's funny. Even the Governor was laughing about it. Mum just gets far too serious about some things."

I was about half way through my third pint when I felt the need to go to the gents. As I was busy relieving myself, a Chinese boy about my age came in and took up station at the urinal to my left. I was totally shocked when his right hand reached out and grabbed my tackle. It was almost a reflex reaction as I swung my right fist, hard into his face. He flew backwards across the narrow room smashing his head against the tiles behind us. It made an awful noise.

I was horrified to see him sliding down the wall, leaving a trail of blood as if a mop had been dipped into red paint and wiped down the bright white tiles. It was horrible!

I quickly did up my fly and made my way back out to our table, trying my best to look cool despite my heart trying its best to explode from my chest.

"C'mon. We've got to get out here fast. I think I just killed a man in the toilet," I hissed as quietly as I could.

"Ha ha ha! You are always the joker!" exclaimed Ragnar.

"I'm not joking, Ragnar. Hurry." I stared at him. He got the message.

He turned to the girls. "He's serious. We'd better go quickly. But act as naturally as you can."

We walked through the raucous crowd and out into the street.

"Let's go to the Godown. I need a whisky."

Chapter Fourteen

I hadn't slept at all, but I had calmed down a lot by the morning when Mum called me for breakfast. Ragnar had gone back to the street outside The Blue Moon and spoken to a British police officer. He had asked what was going on.

The officer had told him that there'd been an altercation between two members of rival Triad gangs. One of them had been left for dead in the toilets, but he had survived. He was in hospital in a critical condition. They knew who was to blame and there was no point in pursuing them.

"We let these gangs fight it out amongst themselves. If they kill each other, we don't care. It's the damage that they do in the community that we care about," he'd told Ragnar.

Ragnar was convinced that they didn't suspect me of any crime.

I was very relieved that the police wouldn't be bothering me. But I was worried about what might happen if some Triad gang thought that I was involved.

Getting down to the Day Centre was a very welcome distraction.

* * * * *

The children arrived and we sang a few songs with them.

After that, I took Knitting over to her horse to build on the great success of the previous day. To my surprise, she kicked it away and held her hands up to me. She said something unintelligible but I understood. She wanted to to walk with me, without her horse.

So that's what we did. After just a few minutes she wriggled her left hand free of mine. We continued to walk around the room with me holding tightly onto her right hand. She was bearing so much weight on her own legs that I almost felt that I could let go.

Knitting obviously felt the same. After a while, she stopped walking and turned her head to glare at me.

"What?" I said.

"Hummah hurr lumph," she said. I could never understand what she was saying, but it meant something to her, and some of the other children seemed to understand what she was saying.

She stood still, refusing to move, and just glaring at me. I knew that something important was whirring around in that head of hers.

Eventually, she slapped my right hand with her left. She looked at me then did it again.

She wanted me to let go.

"Are you sure?"

She nodded vigorously and slapped my wrist again.

The room had fallen silent. All eyes were on us. I looked into her eyes. She was sure.

I let go.

Knitting stood.

Knitting rocked back and forth, swaying like a long grass in a slight breeze.

Then she did it.

She took three rapid steps forward and fell flat on her face.

My jaw dropped. I could hardly believe what I'd just seen. Amazing!

Before I could spring forward to pick her up, she rolled over on to her back and shook her arms and legs in the air, laughing. She laughed loudly and uncontrollably.

"Walk!" she shouted. "WALK!"

I laughed too. And then I burst into tears. My emotions escaped from me like steam from a pressure cooker.

"You walked, Knitting! You actually walked!"

"Walk! Walk!" she cried through her laughter.

Everybody in the room was reacting in their different ways. There was much cheering and clapping and shouting. Mum and Mrs Sutherland-White were crying. Kirsty was hugging herself and looked as if she was about to burst into tears herself.

Knitting was still rolling around on the floor, laughing.

I stepped forward and gathered her up into my arms, hugging her tightly.

She started crying too. Like me, she was shedding tears of happiness.

"Walk," she said again in my ear. It was the first English word she'd ever said to me that I could understand clearly. That word, coming from her lips, was one of the sweetest words I had ever heard.

Our combined joy was boundless.

We held on to each other for two or three minutes.

I turned to face Mum.

"Knitting can walk!" I said. "She can really walk, Mum!"

Mum just grinned at me. It was a huge, genuine grin. I could feel her pride. It was a rare occasion. More than rare: it was unique. A moment that could never be beaten.

That evening, we had a big celebratory dinner at Jimmy's Kitchen.

If I lived to be a hundred, it would be impossible to experience another day as momentous that one had been.

The surgeons said that it was impossible. My own mother didn't believe that it was possible. None of my friends or family believed that it was possible. My best friend, James, told me that he had always believed that it was possible. But really, the only two people in the whole world who had believed were myself and Knitting.

She had achieved something truly remarkable.

That night I went to bed with a voice in my mind shouting at me...

"KNITTING CAN WALK!"

As I dozed off, it occurred to me that Knitting had actually run before she could walk. That thought made me chuckle.

Chapter Fifteen

The next morning, I couldn't wait to get back down to the Day Centre. As soon as the children arrived, I went straight over to Knitting to continue where we'd left off the previous day. Before the morning was over, she'd walked and fallen several times. It must have hurt, but she just would not give up, and I didn't want her to give up either.

When the other children got stuck into painting and piling up building bricks and other activities, Knitting and I carried on with our walking exercises.

Out of the corner of my eye, I noticed Harry Booker talking to my Mum. I waved to him and was slightly bemused when he returned my greeting with a weak smile. He looked very worried.

I started to worry when they left the building together but I just carried on with the working with Knitting until Mum returned about an hour later.

Harry was one of Dad's oldest friends. They had served in the Army together in Borneo in the early sixties. When Dad had left to enter a new career in civil engineering, Harry had joined the Hong Kong Police. He had been serving ever since. We'd had some good times together, including big parties out at the Police Headquarters in Stanley. That's why I was so disturbed by his strange behaviour. By the time Mum returned, I had worried myself into a frenzy. It had to be something to do with the incident at The Blue Moon.

I was right.

Mum called me over.

"We're going for a late lunch with Dad when we're finished here."

"But Mum. I promised James that I'd meet him at the club for a game of squash at two o'clock."

"Forget it. This is serious. I know that you and Kirsty were at that new pub last night when somebody was almost murdered. He may still die. I'm sure you didn't have anything to do with it, but you were there and that could be a big problem. You can go to the club after lunch. Now go back to Knitting, she's looking for you."

Knitting was, indeed, looking for me and smiled at me when I returned to her side. Up went her arms. "Walk," she said. If it was the only word that she ever said that I understood, I would treasure it forever. It was worth more than any fortune.

We had another go on the horse, but it seemed more of a recreational pursuit now, after the events of the previous day. Then we walked around in our usual way, with me holding her outstretched arms and Knitting supporting most of her weight. From time to time, she'd beat my hands away, and take a few unsteady steps before falling over in fits of laughter.

I felt mixed emotions when I finally put her on the minibus and waved goodbye. I was very worried about the seriousness of Mum's invitation to lunch. I had no option to refuse, and what Harry had told her had obviously deeply disturbed her.

Mum refused to tell me anything during the short taxi drive to the Peak tram. Dad was waiting for us and had already ordered me a San Mig and a plateful of spare ribs. Nowhere did spare ribs like Les Quatre Temps. He'd ordered for Mum and Kirsty too. He knew our favourite dishes and drinks.

When we'd settled down and had passed the small talk, Dad became quite solemn.

"Calum. Since Mum called me, I've also spoken with Harry and a few other friends in the police force. You're in trouble."

"Why?"

"It's to do with this chap who was almost killed in the Blue Moon."

"What's that got to do with me, Dad?"

"Well, the police don't think that you had anything to do with it, even though several people saw you leaving the toilets where he was discovered."

"Good!"

"Yes. The victim was a well-known drug dealer and was part of one of the Triad gangs. They believe that he either crossed somebody in his own gang or a rival gang targeted him. Did you see anything?"

I thought long and hard before giving an answer. I chomped messily on another rib.

"Well. Yes. I did see something."

Mum, Dad and Kirsty waited anxiously for my next words.

"I just saw him lying on the floor with blood everywhere. It was all down the wall. I got out of there fast and told the others. Then we left and went to the Godown." I was telling the truth. I hadn't told them any lies. I'd merely missed out what had happened before I saw him lying on the floor. "Anyway, the police don't know much. They told Ragnar that he'd been stabbed. He definitely wasn't stabbed. He'd been beaten up."

"How do you know that?" My sister just had to ask!

Mum interrupted before I could answer. "Never mind that. Listen to your father. It's not the police that you have to worry about."

I looked at Dad, waiting for his explanation.

"The victim is in a critical condition in hospital. The police have questioned members of his own gang and of the rival gang. The big problem for you is that they believe that the gang think it was you who beat up their friend. If they get hold of you, they might kill you."

"I don't believe it."

"Harry does. He advised me that you should leave Hong Kong as soon as possible. And he really means it. He fears for your life."

The blood had drained from Dad's face. I felt queasy myself. He wasn't joking. My world was evaporating. I was genuinely scared, even terrified. Images of the horrible ways that they could kill me were flashing through my mind. Besides, I wasn't due to go back to UK for another six weeks.

Mum explained that Dad had already booked me onto a flight to London the following evening. "I've called Polly, and she's delighted that you'll be staying with her in Perth until you start your Naval training."

"I can't go back yet. Knitting has just started walking. And Iona's Mum has invited me over for Sunday lunch this weekend."

I wasn't even convincing myself, never mind my family.

"Your life is more important than any of that."

Mum was right, of course. Calum the corpse would be incapable of appreciating either a miraculous little girl or a beautiful girlfriend.

The contrast between Hong Kong and Perth could hardly be more extreme. The same could be said about the contrast between hanging around with my friends in this vibrant colony and and a few peaceful weeks being pampered by my lovely Highland grandmother. The latter option had the added appeal of staying alive.

I agreed that I should fly out the following evening and continued to devour my messy ribs. I enjoyed them even more than usual. After all, this could be the last chance I'd ever get to eat ribs at Les Quatre Temps.

The rest of that day and the whole of the next day was like a round of last chance to see and do. I enjoyed every moment to the max. A game of squash with Clive Morris followed by much high jinx at the pool. I still never managed a clean entry into the water for my somersault off the springboard. I was touched as Iona cried when she heard that I was leaving, but this was over-compensated by the most memorable cuddle of my life in the changing rooms.

Although it seemed a bit selfish, I was allowed my choice of dining, for the second evening in a row, at Jimmy's kitchen. After I'd polished off my satellite, George skillfully poured me his famous rainbow: a multi-coloured drink that relied upon his knowledge of the relative specific gravities of the liqueurs that went into the tall, slim glass. And it almost knocked me out.

In the morning, I couldn't stop the flow of tears as I spent almost all of my time at the Day Centre with Knitting. Of course, I spent time with Cheung and Harriet and the rest of the children, and with the other helpers, but it was natural that I should focus on Knitting. I loved that little orphan girl. I admired her courage and determination. She had defied the surgeons who had said that she would never walk. She'd never known that they had passed such a judgement on her, and perhaps that helped. But she had always believed that she would be able to walk, and she'd done it. Not too far, but I was confident that she would continue with her good progress.

Poor Knitting didn't understand why I was crying. She didn't understand that she would never see me again. I did. It was tragic. I was grieving as the minibus departed.

At the airport, I said a sad farewell to my parents and my sister as I headed through the barrier towards security. My Mum warned me that I should not even think of getting off the plane anywhere along the route.

"Your grandmother struggles with the idea of a bus trip to Dundee. The thought of you wandering around some city on the other side of the world would kill her!"

"Don't worry Mum. I will stay on the plane all the way to Heathrow. Then I'll head straight across London to catch the train from Euston to Edinburgh and I'll be on the first train from there to Perth."

"You'd better. And call me as soon as you get to Polly's flat. I don't care what time you call, just call."

"Yes Mum. I promise."

* * * * *

As my plane rose above the waters of the fragrant harbour, I looked across towards the island and picked out our block of flats in Happy Valley. I wondered if I would ever return to this wonderful place.

Epilogue

So much had changed in twenty-five years. I had been looking forward to returning to Hong Kong, but feared that it would have changed beyond all recognition in that time. The trouble was that in the first two days that we'd been there, I'd had no opportunity to find out. It had been just like any other business trip: airport, hotel, office, hotel, office, hotel...

Our schedule meant that we'd be there until at least the weekend, longer if we needed it to complete the work. But today, we had made a big breakthrough. It looked like we had found a resolution to our customer's biggest problem. Their billing run had been over-running into the normal working day and was seriously impacting the performance of the contact centre users. The changes that we'd made meant that the batch program would complete five hours earlier. The customer was very pleased with the result. I was a rather annoyed that they had been ignoring the pleas of one of their junior DBAs who, for the past six months, had been suggesting the exact same solution that we had just implemented. That's the nature of status protocols in some companies, especially in Hong Kong. It would never happen at Summit Software, but things were different in this particular telco.

There were still a few more minor problems to sort out, but the bulk of the work was done. We could take it relatively easy for the rest of the trip. Perhaps I'd be able to take some time out to visit my old haunts.

I put this to my two colleagues, Jagesh and Anders over dinner.

"You two go to the bar. I'm going for a stroll around town for a couple of hours. I might see you later if you're still around when I get back."

"Are you kidding, Calum?" exclaimed Anders. "Have you seen the rain out there?"

"Yes. But it's warm, tropical rain, Anders. It reminds me of my childhood."

"I can empathise with that," chuckled Jagesh. "You Swedish don't know what warm rain is Anders!"

As we'd sat in our taxi on the way to work the last two mornings, and as we'd come in from the brand new, magnificent airport, I'd seen so many changes. When I'd lived in Happy Valley as a teenager, Lan Tau had been a great place to go for a day trip. Its population was probably no more than a few hundred. To me and my sister, it had just been a huge beach. Now it was the gateway to the modern international airport and it had a Disneyland, hotels, lots of big buildings and a causeway connecting it to Kowloon.

The buildings on the mainland and on Hong Kong Island were much taller than when I had last been there in 1974. The Connaught Centre, which had been the tallest building in the colony, was dwarfed by the surrounding skyscrapers. There were flyovers everywhere. Much more land had been reclaimed in the ensuing decades.

Nevertheless, once I started walking around in the rain that evening, I discovered that a lot of the back streets were just as I remembered them. Even some of the shops and restaurants were the same, and I was sure that I recognised a few people.

I decided to walk down Leighton road and see if Sammy's restaurant was still there. And there it was! Even though it was almost eleven o'clock at night, the magnetic pull of curiosity dragged me towards the door. I had a few old photos in my pocket, including some of Sammy, Wei Koo and little Lizzie.

As I entered, one of the waiters came towards me.

"Good evening sir. Is it just..." He stopped in his tracks, his jaw dropping towards the ground. "Calum? Calum? It's you, isn't it? Calum! I don't believe it!"

I recognised him. It was Michael. Still there after all these years. Amazing!

"Michael! How wonderful to see you. I didn't expect to see anyone I knew. I didn't expect the restaurant to be still here. The whole area seems to have been rebuilt."

"Sammy's going to be so annoyed that he missed you. He's just left."

"Sammy's still here too? Wow! Will he be here tomorrow? I'll come back."

"No. I mean yes. Yes, he will be here tomorrow night. But I'll call him now. He'll come straight back."

"There's no need for that. I can come back tomorrow evening, Michael."

I couldn't stop him. Fifteen minutes later, I was sitting at a table with Sammy and Michael, swigging San Mig and reminiscing.

Sammy had found it hard to believe that I had come back after all these years, and he loved the photos. He was such a proud dad and husband. His little girl, who had been a toddler when I last saw her, was now a stewardess with Singapore Airlines. Wei Koo had been to secretarial college and was now the Personal Assistant of the CEO of AIA. Sammy had always been happy in the restaurant and had never had any desire to move anywhere else.

It was almost one o'clock by the time I returned to the hotel, having promised to visit them again before flying back to England. Jagesh and Anders had long since gone to bed.

The next morning, at breakfast, I was full of excitement as I told my friends about the previous evening. They could hardly believe that I'd found people that I'd known so well back in the seventies. To be honest, I was still trying to take it in myself.

"I know that we are supposed to be working, but I am going to take the morning off and leave you two to your own devices. You know what we still need to do. I'll be back with you in the office straight after lunch. I already called Panchali, and she's delighted with the progress that we've made. I just want to go and check out one of my old haunts: a Day Centre for handicapped orphans. I'll be very surprised if it's still there, but you never know."

"A Day Centre for handicapped orphans?"

"Yes. It's a long story. I'll tell you about it this evening. By the way, how do you fancy an Indonesian meal tonight?"

By nine o'clock, I was walking along Queen's Road towards Wanchai Market. Much of what I was seeing was familiar, but there was much more that was totally new to me.

As soon as the church came in to view, I recognised it. I stopped and stared for a few moments. So many memories came flooding back. Eventually, my feet started moving again. I walked down memory lane and in through the door of the hall underneath the church.

It had changed, but only very slightly. It was still full of children and noise, just as it had been the last time I'd walked out of there. The difference was that a small office had been built in the corner. For at least five minutes, I stood and took in the view. I was surrounded by happiness and frantic activity. The children and their helpers were so engrossed in their painting and building and buzzing around that they hardly noticed me. Mum would have been so proud.

A tall, dark lady emerged from the office and made her way over to me.

"Hello. May I help you?"

"Well. I don't know. Erm. Perhaps I should tell you my connection with this place."

"Oh? You have a connection?"

"Yes. This Day Centre was founded by my mother. My name is Calum McDougal, and my mother was . . ."

"Sheena McDougal! Oh my goodness! You're Sheena's son! Wow! I am SO pleased to meet you Calum!"

She was really excited, and I have to admit that it made me feel really good.

"My name is Lydia Schofield. This is such an honour. Come over here Calum. I have something to show you."

She steered me back to the entrance and pointed at a small brass plaque. I read the inscription.

SWALLOWFIELD BAPTIST CHURCH DAY CENTRE
FOR HONG KONG ORPHANS
FOUNDED BY
SHEENA MCDOUGAL
MARGARET SUTHERLAND-WHITE
22 APRIL 1974

My chest filled with pride and my eyes started to fill with tears in memory of my mother. This was a creditable legacy. Lydia could see that I was moved.

"Would you like a coffee? I have a kettle in my office."

Once we were seated and sipping our hot drinks, she started asking me about those early days of the Day Centre. The conversation moved on to the point when I felt compelled to tell her about the day that Knitting took those first steps. As I reached the climax of my story, she actually uttered a stifled squeal.

"That's incredible, Calum!"

Lydia Schofield was a very excitable woman. She'd been on a high ever since I'd first met her.

"I know. I genuinely count it as the greatest achievement of my life. I will never forget the instant that she scrambled those first three steps, even though she fell flat on her face. It was a massive moment for all of us, but especially for me and for Knitting."

"No. You don't understand, Calum. This is much more amazing than you could ever imagine. Come with me."

I hesitated, wondering where she was leading me.

She stood and beckoned me. "This way. Please."

She took me back out into the main hall where the children were still enthusiastically engaged in all sorts of activities. She called across the room.

"Susie. SUSIE!"

A Chinese woman who was busy helping two little boys to build a pile of bricks on a small table looked up.

"Yah?"

"Susie. Come over and meet this gentleman."

Susie stood, picked up her sticks and made her way towards us. When she was about two yards away, she screamed, threw hers sticks to the side and leapt into my arms.

It was her! It was Knitting! It really was Knitting!

"Calum!" she cried.

"Knitting!"

We hugged each other tightly. Tears flowed. We trembled. Lydia was correct. In fact, this was beyond amazing. It was the happiest moment of my life, by far.

I could not believe that here was Knitting; walking, and talking, and hugging me. It really was Knitting. She had come so far in her life. Not only did she recognise me after all these years, as I recognised her, but she was walking and talking. The last time I'd seen her, she could only stagger a few steps and the only English word that I'd heard from her lips was "Walk!"

I was thrilled.

Knitting, or rather, Susie, had grown into a mature woman and was giving back to the community which had given her life and hope as a child. Her achievements, her accomplishments, far exceeded anything that I had ever done in my little life. She was a giant. I could not have been prouder.

Knitting can walk!

She can walk tall: head and shoulders above anybody else whom I have ever known.

A Note from the Author

Thanks for reading *Knitting Can Walk!*

I hope that you enjoyed the story and that the perseverance of Calum and Knitting has inspired you.

You may wish to check out my previous novel, *Eleven Miles*. I aim to write a sequel to that one in the coming year.

Please sign up for my mailing list at http://eepurl.com/bLRZz9 to find out more about my progress and any other writing that I may embark upon in the near future.

In the meantime, if you enjoyed this book, please consider leaving a review on Amazon and Goodreads to help other readers find it. Posting a review only takes a minute but it makes a world of difference!

About the Author

Lance Greenfield writes stories about young, inspirational characters. These stories are based on fact but are mostly fiction.

Connect with Lance: https://lancegreenfield.wordpress.com/
Facebook: https://www.facebook.com/lance.greenfield.37
Twitter: https://twitter.com/lancegmitchell

Printed in Great Britain
by Amazon